# The Portal of ]

Charles Neville Buck

## Alpha Editions

This edition published in 2024

ISBN 9789361478161

Design and Setting By

**Alpha Editions**

www.alphaedis.com

Email - info@alphaedis.com

# Contents

# CHAPTER I

## A VISION UPON A WARNING

The doctor was so small and frail that his narrow face was rescued from inconsequence only by a trimly cropped Van-Dyck with a dignified sprinkling of gray. I always felt that, should I ever see him in a bathing suit, I would have to seek a new physician. I could never again think of him as sufficiently grown-up to practise an adult vocation. Yet when the doctor spoke his mentality issued out of its small habitation of flesh and expanded to commanding proportion.

The little doctor was in fine a very great doctor, and on this occasion he was bullying me with the large authority of a Bonaparte.

"But, Doctor—" I began protestingly.

He raised a small hand which suggested the claw of a delicate bird and fixed me with quizzical eyes that had the faculty of biting sharply through a man's unspoken thoughts.

"Don't assume to say 'but' to me," he sternly enjoined; and since we had long known each other, not only as physician and patient, but also as men who breakfasted at the same hour and the same club table, I momentarily heeded.

"Once upon a time," he continued, "the German Kaiser presumed to question a pilot on his imperial yacht. Do you recall the result?"

"No," said I, "I don't, but——"

Again the doctor eyed me, basilisk fashion, across the bacon and eggs of our belated morning meal, as he continued:

"He very properly reminded the Emperor that upon a vessel in the high seas, a pilot acknowledges no superior this side of Eternity. In matters of health I take the bridge. You obey."

"But—" I weakly insisted.

"You presume to think because you house your nerves in a well-muscled body that they are infallible," he implacably continued. "I've seen rotten motors in excellent garages. I've seen unhappy wives immured in palaces, and I've seen finer figures of men than you in lunatic asylums."

"My nerves are simply of the high-strung type," I argued.

"Those are the kind that snap," retorted the sage. "If you were a racehorse, it might be a matter of reasonable pride to you to be bred in the purple. Being a man with no avocation except the spending of unearned money, it means that you are perilously over-sensitized."

"What unpleasant pedantry are you leading up to?" I demanded. "Out with it."

"I mean to. You have the artistic temperament which, without genius, is worse than useless. You choose to regard yourself a failure and grow morose because you have found the law uncongenial and because editors earn their salaries by returning your manuscripts. The durability of your nervous system depends entirely on how you utilize the next five years."

"Go on," I encouraged him, "don't mind me. Sentence me to death if it amuses you."

"It won't be death, but unless you fortify those nerves," he calmly went on, "there probably will be disaster. It may take any one of several forms."

"As, for instance?" I inquired, with pardonable curiosity.

"Oh, arterio-sclerosis, paralysis, insanity, something of that sort."

"Thank you kindly," I murmured, as I reached for the matches. "Can I have my choice of the lot?"

"However," went on the big little doctor, "if you devote the next few years to a program of diversified travel, you ought to lay up an account of nerve-strength upon which you can draw *ad lib.* for forty or fifty years to come. You should even have a surplus against the unfortunate exigency of living on when you are old and useless."

"But I have traveled," I argued. "I've been to———"

He interrupted me with a snort, and swept my declarations aside, unfinished.

"You have dabbled at travel, like a school-girl nibbles at chocolates. Get out on the hike and stay out for a year or two. Build into your artificial self something of the out-door animal. You have a fair start—you were once an athlete." He rose to go down to his motor, and I shouted after him contemptuous and profane criticism. Nevertheless within the week I booked passage for the Mediterranean.

I found once more that Europe and the African fringe of the land-locked sea have to offer to the hunger of the wanderlust only a stereotyped table-d'hôte. Shortly it cloys. Within several weeks one thing only had promised to break the stagnant surface with a riffle of interest. And that one thing puzzled me in no small degree, since it was not such a matter as would ordinarily have challenged my attention. I have passed with a glance many beautiful women, and felt no need to turn my head for a further inspection. I am not of the cavaliering type, and yet here I was finding myself interested, in a strange and indefinable way, in a woman whose face I had not seen, and whose name I did not know. That, I told myself, was the secret of it. It was exactly because she was elusive, mysterious in fashion, that I found my flat interest piqued. I never had more than the swish of her skirt or a glimpse of her retreating figure, until it came about that sheer inquisitiveness gave her an augmented importance. At all events, she had eluded me over southern Europe from Genoa to Constantinople, and thence into Egypt, and I wanted to see her face. It was at Naples that I had my first hasty and imperfect view of her. I was hurrying through the Galeria Umberto, on my way to a luncheon appointment for which I found myself late. As I passed Merola's a young woman was sitting before a counter, with her back to the street, trying on gloves. I could appreciate the gypsy grace of her figure, which was slender, because one of the avocations into which I have essayed without distinction is painting. The single thing at which I have not failed, except the success of having selected parents who bequeathed me money, is an appreciation of the beautiful. That appreciation, despite my hurry, brought me to a stop for a full glance at her; but there was no mirror at any part of the shop which gave me a reflection of her averted face, and as my appointment was imperative, I refrained from going in to buy gloves. But there was something so exquisite in her bearing, and in the tasteful lines of her simple traveling gown, that I caught myself thinking of her. Then as I went down to the quay a day later to say farewell to some friends, just as the gangplank of an outgoing steamer was about to be drawn up, I saw her hurrying across it. Her face was still averted. I strained to catch a feature, but a wayward gust of bay breeze wrapped a filmy veil about the profile which was for a moment turned my way—and hid it. She did not house at the deck rail but disappeared as the gangplank came up and cut off pursuit. But I had added to my first impression the knowledge that she did not merely walk. She soared as though her feet were the sandals of Hermes, and she carried herself with the splendid grace of a slender young queen.

---

**A young woman was sitting before a counter, with her back to the street, trying on gloves.**

---

The luncheon appointment, which had thwarted my impulse to turn into the glove shop, and so end the mystery in its incipiency, brought a long trail of complications and caused me to envy those fortunate men who are not handicapped by the possession of relatives. I have sometimes thought that the truly ideal existence would be to be born an orphan unhampered by cousins, aunts or any of those human beings who are privileged to make demands upon our times and thoughts.

From the moment when I watched the skyline of New York sink slowly behind the horizon until I reached Naples I had at least been a free agent. But hardly had I signed my guest card at Parker's Hotel and strolled out to hail a crazy Neapolitan hack when the angular and purposeful figure of my Aunt Sarah loomed up in the near foreground and—saving her grace—eclipsed the picturesqueness of the town and the distant cone of Vesuvius. I had known vaguely that this estimable lady was beating her way about Europe, guide-booked and grimly set upon self-improvement, but I had hoped to keep the area of two or three monarchies between us.

I knew that from one to the other of the Cook's Agencies she would be flitting with the same frantic energy that characterizes the industry of the ant. That I should myself pass within hailing distance of her party or be recruited in her peregrinations was a disaster which I had not anticipated. None the less the blow had fallen and I had walked unwarned into the ambuscade of her fond embrace. Aunt Sarah would now converse voluminously of cathedrals and old masters, and all the things upon which tourists are fed to a point of acute mental dyspepsia.

She had ordered me to luncheon with much the same finality as that with which royalty commands the attendance of guests at court. I had gone meekly though doing so involved passing Merola's and opened up a series of events which were destined to alter for the worse my immediate future. But the luncheon had been only the beginning, and greater misfortunes were to follow in due order.

I have never since been able to understand precisely what form of paresis seized upon me, and paralyzed my normally efficient power of lying, when she instructed me to attach myself to her party for a motor trip to Villefranche and Nice. I do know that no available mendacity occurred to my shocked brain and I found myself murmuring an acceptance. The acceptance was again meek and spineless. I had discovered at luncheon that Aunt Sarah, with that motherly obsession which appears to characterize many maiden ladies of fifty and beyond, had under wing a party of three young ladies who were capping off their educations with the post graduate "advantages" of the grand tour. That these young ladies possessed all the homely virtues, I have not the slightest doubt. Their faces and figures attested the homeliness and their virtue was such that they seemed always wondering whether their halos were on straight. Theirs was an insatiate greed for intellectual feeding. They browsed through their Baedeckers with a seeming terror lest something erudite escape them. They pursued and captured and assimilated every fleeting fact which might improve their minds. Until my captivity they had no man with their party. That was probably because Aunt Sarah had made the strategic mistake of permitting all those, whom she might otherwise have annexed, to see her girls. She should have enlisted her male escort first and held back the introductions until desertion was impracticable. At all events, I had, like the imbecile I was, "fallen for it," and surrendered my liberty. When the boat bearing the unknown divinity set sail I was merely a satellite of Aunt Sarah's constellation and no longer a free agent.

Because I happened to be, in a superficial way, familiar with the tourist-tramped sections of the Continent, I became a sort of gentleman courier, without recompense, and because I had once undertaken to be a painter, I was expected to give extemporaneous lectures on the art treasury of the museums. We walked several thousand miles, or maybe it was millions, over those peculiarly hard floors which make art galleries penitential institutions. I saw the three plain faces in every phase of soulful rapture that can be elicited by the labors of the masters, from Michelangelo to Murillo.

When this had gone on for several centuries, or maybe it was æons, I discovered that every art gallery has two or three truly interesting features, though the full enjoyment of these was denied me. I speak of the exits. Perhaps to the unintimidated mind of the outsider it may appear that whatever agonies I underwent were the deserved result of my own abjectness. It is easy to say that I might have pleaded other plans and gone on my way enfranchised. To such a critic my only and sufficient reply is that he or she does not know my Aunt Sarah. My Aunt Sarah says to whomsoever she chooseth, "Go," and he goeth; "Come," and he cometh. She knew perfectly well that I had no other plans. She correctly assumed me to be a derelict floating without purpose and with my chart lost over-side. She virtuously resolved that for once I should be made of use, in assisting to improve the minds of the three plain young ladies. Lying would have been quite futile. Consequently she said, "Come," and I came. When I learned that we were to make the tour to the Riviera towns by motor, I welcomed the suggestion as a less evil than cathedrals and art galleries. At least we should be out of doors and in the exhilaration of rapid motion one might hope to forget the three young ladies at brief and blessed intervals. One could not at the same time think of the culture-pursuing trio and anything rapid.

It has been my curse in life that I have dabbled at so many things that I can be made of smattering use in almost any circumstance. Our chauffeur discovered this three and one-half minutes after the occurrence of our first blow-out, when Aunt Sarah, taking pity upon his sweating and dust-grimed brow, told me off to help him patch the puncture. After that it was impossible to feign ignorance as to the interior workings and deviltries of motor cars.

The Upper Corniche Road is perhaps the most charming driveway of the world—and I say this with due reverence to Amalfi. By a road as white as a fresh tablecloth and as smooth as a bowling alley one speeds to the purring of his motor along the way thrown up for the tramping feet of Bonaparte's battalions. From a commanding height the traveler looks down, as from the roof of the world, with close kinship of peaks and clouds, upon a panorama a-riot with breadth and depth and color. Fascinating road-houses of stucco walls curtained behind a profusion of clambering roses tempt one to pause and take his ease to the tinkle of guitars and mandolins. But Aunt Sarah and the girls, ever bent upon reaching the next cathedral with a stained glass window or the next dingy canvas of a saint sitting on a cloud, were scarcely amenable to the lure of road-house temptation.

They seemed to regard Europe as a transitory effect which might fade like the glories of sunset before they had finished seeing it, and anything savoring of the dilatory aroused their suspicion.

Far below us lay the outspread Mediterranean, blue beyond description and upon her placid bosom sailboats shrunk to the size of swallows and yachts seemed no larger than nursery toys.

One gracious afternoon, while I was occupying the front seat beside the driver, I almost attained a state of contentment. I was pretending that I had forgotten all about the human freight in the tonneau. My eyes were drinking in the smiling beauty framed by the wide horizon, when suddenly the droning of the motors fell quiet and with no warrantable reason the automobile slid to a halt and declined to proceed farther.

# CHAPTER II

## PURSUING A WILL-O'-THE-WISP

Aunt Sarah and the girls were much annoyed and their annoyance did not grow less when, after a half-hour of diagnosis, the chauffeur emerged, grease-stained and exhausted from under the car, shaking his head. He frankly admitted that his worm's eye view had failed to enlighten him as to the trouble. Aunt Sarah turned upon me eyes mirroring a faith sufficient to move even stalled motor cars.

"I am sure, my dear," she said, sweetly, "your mechanical aptitude can find a remedy for this difficulty."

It was, of course, an order to burrow into the confined space between the road bed and the bottom of the car, and of course I burrowed. For a time I was out of touch with all matters transpiring in the great outer world, but finally I saw the inverted face of our chauffeur gazing in upon me and heard his bellowing voice. I have hitherto neglected to mention that our chauffeur was neither French nor Italian, but Irish. He was, in fact, an excellent fellow, and the only member of our party whom I found companionable.

"Sure, sor," he yelled, "there's another car in trouble just around th' turn av' th' road."

I supposed that he was imparting this information only out of the assumption that misery loves company, and inasmuch as my reply was profane, it need not be quoted. In a moment more, however, his grinning visage reappeared at the road level. "They wants to know if you can't be afther lending 'em a tire-iron?"

"What do they think this is?" I roared back, squirming far enough to clear my face for utterance, but not far enough to see what was going on. "This isn't a repair crew."

It was hardly a gracious response to a fellow motorist in trouble, but my point of view was oppressed with the weight of a paralyzed car, and Aunt Sarah and the girls, and I was misanthropic to the degree of sourness. From my position whatever conversation ensued was merely an incoherent babble of voices. Palpably, despite my discourtesy, Mr. Flannery had supplied the inquirers with whatever they needed, and they had gone their way. I, in the course of the next few minutes, emerged from my hedge-hog isolation, tinkered with the carburetor, and crawled back again into concealment. Then someone returned the borrowed tire-iron. I did not have the opportunity to speak to the Someone, and I should not have seen the Someone at all had I not happened to catch the shouted words of Mr. Flannery. Mr. Flannery had so accustomed himself to pitting his voice against machinery that even in moments of quiet he hurled his words like the roar of a bull. So, as he spoke now to the unknown person, I recognized an allusion to myself. The words which set me to extricating myself as speedily as possible from my humble position were as follows:

"Sure, ma'am, th' boss would be afther bein' more polite to yer, only the car is layin' a little heavy on his stummick, and it gives him a bit of a grouch."

The word which excited me was the "ma'am," and my excitement was no means allayed when I stood clear in the road and saw just disappearing around a curve a figure which I recognized. It could be no other figure, for no other figure that I had ever seen could walk with the same triumphant and lissome grace. Again the face was turned away from me, and about her hat floated a confusing cloud of veil. But she had been there within a few feet and possibly had even heard my surly responses to her request for assistance. Possibly she had seen my wriggling feet while I, who would have esteemed it the greatest possible privilege to have assisted her in any way, had lain there surrounded by dust and profanity. I was seized with a mad impulse to run after her, but I knew that the return of my iron signified that their tire-mending was finished and they were on their journey.

My own repairs were not finished, and I stood there with streaks of grease across my face, caked with dust and by no means presenting the appearance with which a man might hope to appear acceptable in the eyes of divinity. Aunt Sarah and her bevy of young intellectuals, I found, had withdrawn to the greater comfort of a near-by road-house, and could give me no information, while Flannery's description was on the whole, unsatisfactory. The idiot had not asked her name, and in answer to all my questions could only assure me vaguely that the young lady was "a peach." One thing he had noticed. The car, which had passed us a quarter of an hour before was a large blue touring car, of high horse-power. It is strange what details impress certain minds and what goes unseen. So again I had missed my chance, and the incident had not served to reconcile me to my serfdom.

Several days later I had succeeded in gaining a brief leave of absence from my duties as courier, and was spending an interval of sadly needed rest.

I had the hope that the unknown girl and her party would be stopping for a while in one of the closely grouped towns along the coast: Nice, Cannes, Mentone, Monte Carlo—it mattered little which one it might be. If she was in any of these, I should eventually find her, and I haunted the dazzling whiteness of the Boulevard des Anglais, with a buoyant pulse beat of expectancy. At any moment I might again catch a glimpse of her in a shop or café, and if I did, I meant that it should be more than a glimpse, and that she should not again escape until I had at least seen her face. I spent most of my time wondering what she was like. Would the full view bring a greater sense of fascination or the pang of disillusionment? It might be that when I saw her I should find myself harshly awakened from a dream, but at all events, there would be certainty, and an end to the tantalizing sense of following a will-o'-the-wisp which constantly eluded. She gave me one very anxious afternoon. I had been taking a horseback ride near town when I came upon a wrecked and empty automobile. The physical facts showed clearly what had happened. The car had evidently skidded while speeding, in an effort to turn out for some passing vehicle, and had tried to climb a stone wall. There must have been a very ugly moment, as the twisted front wheels and crumpled hood attested. What frightened me was the fact that it was a large, blue touring car of the same sort, if not identical, with the one described by Flannery. I was commencing my ride when I saw it, but I turned back at once to town and began an investigation. I finally learned that the chauffeur for a local garage had taken a party of his own friends for a joy ride, and that the expedition had come to summary grief. My effort to trace the history of that particular car for a week or two past resulted in nothing. I was informed that it had been hired many times and to many unrecorded persons, usually for the afternoon or day.

Several nights later I was sitting at a roulette table in Monte Carlo's *Cercle des Etrangers*. I had fallen in with a coterie of chance acquaintances, who for some reason held faith in my luck and insisted upon my crowding into a vacant place at the wheel. My function was to submit to the issue of fortune not only my own stack of *louis d'or*, but also the considerable purse that they had raised among them.

My table was near the center of the main *salle*, and at my elbows crowded the little party of men and women whose interests hung upon my success or failure. It was the same old scene; the same old life that one sees year after year in this chief cathedral of the gods of chance. Men and women from both hemispheres stood or sat in the tense absorption of eyes riveted on dancing ball and whirling disc. At my right was a regally gowned woman whose delicate features were now as hard as agate and whose eyes were avid. At my left was a saturnine Spaniard who smiled indifferently, but who did not know his cigar had died to a stale coldness. I was experiencing the sense of disillusionment which invariably comes to me afresh when I enter the Casino of Monaco. I always ascend the stairs of the palace which the principality-supporting syndicate has provided for its patrons with a mild elation of expectancy. I always take my place at the tables with the realization of disappointment. The sparkle of jewels is there; sometimes the beauty is there, but the spirit that rules is not a spirit of gaiety; and the glitter of eyes makes me forget the diamonds. The cold lust of greed flashes in the hard brightness of set faces.

Between the droning announcements of the croupier insidious thoughts force themselves. I think of the management's efficient ambulance services; of the exhaustive arrangements by which unknown patrons may be promptly identified; and the sinister discoveries of the beach. These things were in my mind now as the stack of gold pieces at my front alternately piled and dwindled under a fitful sequence of petty losses and gains.

I may have been at the table an hour when I began to have the insistent feeling of someone in particular standing at my back. Of course, there were many people behind me. Besides my own party was the crowd of idle onlookers as well as others who were impatiently waiting to seize upon vacant places about the board.

And yet, just then I could not turn my head. My system involved leaving the winnings upon the table for three successive spins of the wheel. I had played a group of numbers in the black, cautiously avoiding the alluring perils of the greater odds, and twice my little pile of *louis d'or* had drawn in its prize money. On the third spin we stood to lose the entire amount of our augmented stake or see our pile swell commandingly. While I waited for the croupier to close the betting and touch the button, I twisted my head backward, to determine whose presence in the throng had so subtly announced itself to my consciousness. But the barrier of faces that pressed close against my chair cut off all who stood further back. The wheel raced; the ball danced madly about its rim; the crowd stood bating its breath; and the scattered piles of gold lay in doubt on the green baize diagram.

It was over. The croupier sang out the winning number, column and combinations. The rake was extended to push over to me a fairly imposing pile of French gold. I was conscious of coming in for more than my individual share of interest. Luck had been with me, and at Monte Carlo, the lucky man is the man of moment. But the sense of some personality above the many personalities was now borne in upon me with irritating force. I was impatient to rise and push back my chair and look about me, but as I attempted to do so, the men and women whose capital I had increased raised a chorus of remonstrance. I reluctantly resumed the place which I had been about to abdicate and once more laid out my stake. This time I pushed the entire pile out onto the green cloth in a pyramid on the black. I knew if I lost it they would willingly surrender my services. Even at that cost I wanted freedom.

For, in the moment that I had been standing there, I had caught a glimpse of a retreating figure, which disappeared through the door, almost at the instant that my eyes identified it. It was the figure of a woman in evening-dress, or rather, I should say, of *the* woman in evening-dress. There was the same graceful majesty of bearing, the same slim grace—and the same averted face. But because I wished to leave the table fortune pursued me. Spin after spin doubled, tripled, quadrupled my swelling pile of money. Finally I told them that I would remain for three more tests of chance—but no more. I could hardly abandon these enthused men and women without warning, but as soon as I had fulfilled the obligation, I rose, and I fear there was more of precipitate haste than of courtesy in my manner of shouldering my way through the press of onlookers, to the door and the wonderful embroidery of flower beds before the casino. Eyes followed me, for my luck had held and I was a momentary sensation. It was still early, as hours go in a place where the major activity belongs to night life, and for two hours I haunted the cafés and boulevards without result. The next day proved equally fruitless, but that night, as I was idling with my after-dinner cigar, along the Boulevard de Condemine, I saw strolling at some distance ahead of me, a young man and a girl. It was she, and I had only to hasten my steps to overtake and see her. I could guess that the man with her was a Frenchman. The cut of his clothes and the jaunty swagger of his bearing were distinctively Gallic. My imagination could read the title "fortune hunter" as though it were embroidered on his coat-tails.

I was resentful, and hurried on, but as usual I was destined to disappointment. An untimely and inconsequential acquaintance loomed up in my path, and when I attempted to brush hastily by him, he slapped me on the back and hailed me with that most irritating of all conceivable forms of address, "Well, how is the boy to-night?"

He did not find the "boy" particularly affable that night, but with an accursed and persistent geniality he succeeded in delaying me for the space of a few precious moments. At a distance, I saw her disappear into a lighted doorway against which her face and figure showed only in silhouette. Again I had lost her. I could hardly pursue her into the entrances of private houses, but I noted the location and went back to my apartments in the Hotel Hermitage with the comforting thought that we were in the same town and that by rising early the next morning, and searching tirelessly till midnight, I should ultimately be able to see her.

Before sleep came to me a telegram was brought to my door.

Aunt Sarah had succeeded in becoming involved in some ludicrous difficulty with the Italian customs officials. She implored that I come at once to her rescue. How she had achieved it, was a matter of inscrutable mystery. I had always found the politeness of Italian customs officers as gracious as a benediction, but Aunt Sarah was a resourceful person. I rejoined her detestable cortège long enough to extricate her from her newest difficulty, and to discuss with her her plans for the immediate future. I found that she and her young ladies were yearning for the sepia tinted walls of Rome where, under every broken column and crumbling arch their hungry souls might drink deep draughts of improving tradition and culture. I knew that they would waste no time musing by moonlight in the shadows of the Colosseum, but that with Latin dictionaries they would decipher in the broad light of day the inscriptions on the arcs of Titus and Constantine. None the less, I encouraged their idea and enlarged upon the suitability of this time. I looked up the train schedules and wired for hotel reservations. Every moment that they hesitated I was excitedly quoting, though not aloud, lines that came back from the days of a less-mature literary taste:

"'Why dost thou stay and turn away,Here lies the path to Rome.'"

I thought it the part of wisdom to refrain from mentioning until the actual moment of their departure that my own way lay in an opposite direction. But when I had seen them settled in their first-class compartments and the accommodating guard had reassured me by locking them in, I turned with a sigh of contentment and fled back to Monte Carlo. I had been absent only a few days, but I returned to a dusty and desolate town. Perhaps the numbers of gamblers and pleasure-seekers had not actually diminished. Perhaps they had even increased, but a day's search satisfied me that the unknown lady had gone, and for me the town was empty.

What idiosyncrasy drove me to the Holy Land, I cannot say, unless it was that after my exhausting term of cathedral inspection I felt a desire to have a look at that temple which, except for the Taj Mahal, has always appealed to me as the world's most beautiful place of worship—the Mosque of Omar.

Riding one day on a donkey around the walls of Jerusalem, I had a glimpse of Her standing on the ramparts above me by the gate of the Needle's Eye. But as I looked up, the sun was full in my eyes and I could distinguish only the lashing of her skirts in the wind, and a halo-like aura of gold about her head, which was uncovered. At that distance her face was a featureless oval. Until night came with its howling of a thousand dogs I visited the places to which guides most frequently conduct their charges. But in the Temple of The Sepulchre, on the Mount of Olives, at the Jews' Wailing Place and among the vaulted bazaars, there was only failure for my quest. For two days I hunted, and while I hunted she must have gone down to Jaffa or departed for the overland trip to Syria.

# CHAPTER III

## I EMBARK ON A FOOL'S ERRAND

I was sitting on the terrace at Shepheard's Hotel on the evening of my arrival there. I was finding life flat, as one must who can discover no fascination in Cairo's appeal to the eyes, nostrils and ears. Before me was the olla-podrida of touring fashion and fellaheen squalor; the smell of camels and attar of roses; the polyglot chatter of European pleasure-seekers and the tom-toms of Arab pilgrims.

Then once more I saw her. But still I did not see her face. I suppose there were other persons with her. I did not notice. I did notice the salient thing. She was boarding a motor 'bus, presumably for the Alexandria train, and was followed by the usual Cairene retinue of tarbooshed porters and luggage-bearers.

My glimpse of her was again only in exit. My baggage had just been unpacked, and I also could not catch the Alexandria train. I had been foolish enough to announce my coming by postcard from Jerusalem to an acquaintance at the Turf Club and had found awaiting me at Shepheard's on my arrival a note informing me that George Clann, a friend of past days, had invited a few army officers and native men for dinner that evening to meet me. The note added that no excuse would be accepted. I had called up the club and signified my acceptance. That was before I had seen the departing goddess, but I was due in the Sharia el Magrabi an hour hence and so was once again completely anchored.

Had I seen her in entrance instead of in exit only, I should perhaps have remained in Egypt and fanned into rebirth a languid interest in sarcophagi and cartouches and camel-riding and scrambling up the comfortless slants of pyramids.

As it was I began to subscribe to the Oriental idea of an inevitable destiny. I admitted to myself that it was written that for me this lady was to remain as unseen as though she belonged to the latticed and veiled seclusion of some pasha's harem. I told myself that had my first glimpse been a full one I should have gone on my way with prompt forgetfulness and that a curiosity so strange and fantastic must influence me no further.

I sought out an empty place on the terrace where unintentionally enough I overheard an earnest conversation between a fair-haired and enthusiastic young Englishman and a grizzled fellow in middle life. They were talking business in one of the writing-rooms which give out through open windows upon the terrace, and the enthusiasm of the younger gave a carrying quality to his voice.

He was, it appeared from his solicitude, seeking a billet which it lay in the power of his elder vis-à-vis to bestow. From the discussion which neither of them treated as confidential I learned that there is somewhere in the Pacific Ocean a perfectly useless island from which certain ethnological data and exhibits might be obtained. It further appeared that the British Museum was deficient in these particular curios and that the glass cases were yearning to be filled. The youth had been employed in Soudanese excavations and research. Now that work had ended and with it the pay, the necessity for other work and pay had not ended.

"The billet down there," suggested the elder man, "will be no end beastly, I dare say. A tramp steamer sails from Port Said in three days for Singapore, Sandakan and the South Seas. The pay will be one hundred and fifty pounds for the job. The fare will probably be maggoty biscuits—still, if you feel game to have a dash at it——" The speaker finished with a shrug which seemed to add, "It's never difficult to find a fool."

But the young man laughed with a whole-hearted enthusiasm, that entirely missed the under note of contempt in the manner of his benefactor. "Well, rather," he declared. "And I say, you know, its jolly good of you, sir."

Later I made the acquaintance of the young Briton in the American bar where over Scotch and soda we discussed the project, to the end that I nominated and elected myself an assistant forager for the British Museum, serving at my own expense. There was something likeable about my new and naïve acquaintance, who was so eager to shoulder his futile way across a third of the globe's circumference in search of crudely inscribed rocks and axe-heads and decaying skulls. My own experience in life had been even more futile. I had learned to speak five languages and had completely failed of gaining a foothold in five useful professions: Art, Law, Literature, Music and Contentment. Possibly the appeasement of my Salatheal hunger, the curing of the curse, did not after all lie along the routes of Cunarders and Pullmans. Maybe I was still nibbling at travel as the school-girl nibbles at chocolates. Perhaps his method of taking the long and empty trail was the heroic medicine my itching feet required. At all events, I sententiously quoted to myself, "I think It will kill me or cure, and I think I will go there and see."

When I informed young Mansfield, for that proved to be his name, that I meant to be his traveling companion, his almost childlike face took on an incredulous expression. He was a great two-hundred-pound chap whose physique should logically have been the asset of a pirate or a pugilist, but the visage which surmounted it had a rosy pinkness and his blue eyes wore the guileless charity of essential innocence. With his physical power went a long-suffering good nature, and as he talked of the widely scattered places he had seen and the things which should have made him wise in his generation it seemed to me that his soul must have worn a macintosh, from which the showers of experience had been shed off without leaving a mark. I have seen mastiffs with eyes full of wistfulness because Nature has denied their affectionate temperaments the gentle lives of lap dogs. Mansfield struck me the same way. Why a man, by his spare and simple standards as rich as Cr[oe]sus, should care to ship with him on a voyage promising maggoty biscuits, was quite beyond his mental process. He confessed, in all frankness, that he did it merely for the money—the pitiful hundred and fifty. There was a girl back in England, probably as devoid of surprises and complications of character as a lane-side primrose. I pictured her to myself as a creature of pink and shallow prettiness. The day to which his ambition strained as the ultimate goal was the day when he could become a curator in the British Museum and transplant her to decent London lodgings. He longed to placard and arrange scarabs in a plate-glass case and to classify Chimbote pottery and on bank holidays to push a go-cart in the park.

I was glad, however, when I went over the rust-red side of the *Wastrel* that Mansfield went with me. We had known that we were shipping on a mean vessel, and one shouldered out of more orderly chartings, because of her unworthiness. Liners did not ply the tepid waters for which we were bound: waters ridden by no commerce save the peddling of copra and pearl shell and beche-de-mer. Yet even the warning had not prepared me for what I found, as I first stepped upon her unclean decks and had my initial view of her more unclean crew. Perhaps there are other corroded hulks shambling here and there among the less frequented ports of the seven seas as uninviting in appearance and as villainously manned as was the *Wastrel*, but on this point I stand unconvinced. A glance told us that her sea-worthiness was questionable and that her over-burdening cargo pressed her Plimsoll mark close to the water line. We were to learn by degrees that her timbers were rotten, her plates rust-eaten and her engines junk. Her officers were outcasts from respectable seafaring, none too cordial in their relations with admiralty courts. They had fallen back on the hazardous command of such a vessel as this not from choice, but necessity, precisely as other types of unemployed and hopeless men fall back on vagrancy and crime. Her crew was picked from the dregs of scattered ports. They were Lascars, Kanakas, Chinese and non-descripts from here and there; haled forth and signed from dives where human garbage trickles down to the sea. At first they interested me as new and roughened types of men, yet as I say, I was more than grateful for the shoulder touch of at least one being of my own sort. From our arrival, none of them except the captain and officers took the slightest pains to conceal that they regarded us as unwelcome interlopers and even the courtesy of the after-guard was short-lived enough. In that desert of taciturnity Mansfield babbled like a brook and overflowed with young sentimentality.

The first leg of our journey ended at Borneo, leaving us as unacquainted with officers and seamen, save in the surface details of personal appearance, as we had been at Port Said. Now we were dropping Sandakan harbor over the stern. Already the sprawling, hillside town, framed in its mangrove swamps, was lost around the buttress of the harbor's sentinel rock. Ramparts of sandstone were burning with a ruddy glow in the sunset.

A sense of isolation settled on us. As we had nosed our way outward Mansfield had been leaning silently on the after rail. His eyes had dwelt lingeringly on the green gardens and white walks of the British Consulate which sits upon its hill. Now we had seen the last of that and of the bay's flotilla of matting-sailed junks. Off the port bow were only beetling sandstone and the countless gulls, flashing white as they tilted the snowy linings of their wings into the sun. He talked for a time, in low tones of the girl in Sussex as men will talk when they are homesick, and then he rather shamefacedly produced from somewhere and opened at random a much battered blank-book, written in a woman's hand.

"I dare say," he hesitantly told me, "I have no moral right to read this. It's quite personal, yet it's unsigned. Invasion of privacy can't apply to anonymous persons, you know." He paused for a minute and indolently watched the screaming hordes of Sandakan birds as if awaiting my agreement, but I said nothing.

"You see," he continued, "I've been living lately in a cheap *pension* at Cairo and, before that, in beastly Soudan inns, so when I drew a bit in advance I resolved to treat myself to a day or two at Shepheards. You remember how full the house was? They had to give me a small room on the roof. It was really a sort of servant's room in less crowded times, I fancy. A beggar of an Arab used to pray on his rug in front of my door.... In rummaging about I found this." He held up the blank-book. "I looked for an address, meaning to post it to its owner but there was no address and only given names— there's not a surname between these covers. Some servant must have found it in a vacated room and later left it in the one to which I had fallen heir. Seems to have been some girl's desultory but intimate diary. Just an entry now and then, with evidently long gaps between. You see the first writing is immature, almost childish—and the last is dated at Cairo."

I nodded my head, but said nothing. He appeared deeply interested but his simple punctilio required the reinforcement of my approval, before he could quite clear the skirts of his conscience in the matter of having sampled its contents.

"You see," he half-apologized, "my first glance was disinterested, I was merely seeking to identify ownership. But from just a few lines, read in that fashion, I saw that it was—" his voice became serious, almost awed—"well that it was rather wonderful. Some girl has been putting her heart into words here—" he tapped the blank-book—"and she's written a genuine human document." Again he paused, drumming on the rail with the fingers of one hand.

"From a half-dozen bits of Chimbote pottery," he reflected, "I can read a great deal of the habits and life of the Incas. I can restore an extinct mammal from some fragments of skeleton, but I find it jolly difficult to understand anything about a woman. If a fellow means to marry he ought to try to understand. That's why I'd like to have a dip into this. Do you think I might?"

"Do you think," I countered, smiling, "that you would have the right to read somebody's unsigned love-letters?" A certain magazine editor had once witheringly opined that I would never succeed in literature until I acquired some insight into the feminine riddle. But he had not pointed me to diaries. He had bluntly advised me to fall in love with a few variant types.

Until a man had found blond or dark hairs on his coat shoulder, said the editor, he could not hope to write about heartbeats. If he had found various kinds, and that often, he could write better.

Young Mansfield was giving my question a graver and more literal consideration than it merited.

"I rather think," he said seriously, "that one might read such letters. Unless the offense is against some definite person there is no offense at all."

"Perhaps you are right," I admitted, with a listless avoidance of argument, and in a moment more he had opened the book at random and was reading aloud.

# CHAPTER IV

## SOME PASSAGES FROM A DIARY

Mansfield was right. The pages of this diary struck the essentially human note of frank self-avowal. They were as fragrant as May orchards, their sweetness of personality made one think of brave young dreams among dewy blossoms. But I confessed to him the feeling that we were trespassers into these secrets, and after that he either laid the book by altogether or read it only when alone.

The *Wastrel* was cruising at her cripple's pace southeast by east, through those hot waters which lie directly above the equator. After some days we sloped across the line, but still clung to the hideous swelter of the next meridian. Our course lay among groups of lush islands which simmered in steam and fever, and the merciless, overhead sun beat upon us, as if focused through a burning glass until the pitch oozed from the deck cracks, and the sweat from our pores, and the self-control from our curdled tempers. Faces that had been sullen at Sandakan grew malevolent and menacing at 150 degrees, east, where, if I remember rightly, we crossed the equator.

The scowls of the men dwelt hatefully upon Captain Coulter as he paced the bridge. From scraps of information picked up here and there in fo'castle disparagement, I pieced together a lurid abstract of his history. I knew how wild and unsavory were the reputations of many of the men of the eastern beaches. I had listened to tales of *lanai* and *bund*, but even in such company our skipper stood out as uniquely wicked.

The sheer and hypnotic force of his masterful will lay over and silenced the ship. From the first, he dominated. But if he had dominated at the latitude of 120 he domineered at 150, and to this domineering he brought all those extremes of tyranny which lie at the hand of a ship's captain on the high seas. At times the sheer, undiluted brutality of this control compelled my unwilling admiration. Every pair of eyes that met his from the fo'castle, were eyes of smoldering hatred and fear, and though he assumed scornful unconsciousness of this attitude, he knew that his security was no greater than that of the lion-tamer, whose beasts have begun to go bad. He must appear to invite attack, and upon its first intimation of outbreak, he must punish, and punish memorably.

Captain Coulter was little above the average in physical pattern and he walked with a slight defect of gait, throwing one foot out with an emphatic stamp. His face was always clean-shaven, and it might have served a sculptor for a type of the uncompromising Puritan, so hidden were its brutalities and so strong its note of implacable resoluteness.

Over a high and rather protrusive forehead, long hair of iron gray was always swept back. Bushy and aggressive brows shaded eyes singularly piercing and of the same depth and coldness as polar ice. His nose was large and straight, and his lips set tight and unyielding like the jaws of a steel trap. The chin was square and close-shaven. Our captain was a silent man, yet in his own fashion bitterly passionate. Heffernan, the first mate, was a tawdry courtier, who studiously considered his chief in every matter, and maintained his position of concord by ludicrous care to risk no disagreement. In the stuffy cabin where three times a day we sweltered over bad food Mansfield and I studied the attitudes of the officers.

Coulter grimly amused himself over his eating by making absurd statements for the sheer pleasure of seeing his next in command, fall abjectly into agreement. The second mate, however, was impenetrably silent. He was without fear, but a life which had evidently brought him down a steep declivity from a lost respectability, had taught him consideration for odds. If he did not contradict the dogmatic utterances of his chief in table conversation, he at least refused to agree.

Mansfield and I were convinced that if this prematurely gray fellow with the dissipated face, cut in a patrician mould, could ever be brought to the point of personal narrative, he would have a stirring story to tell. We also knew that he would never tell it.

Once before the feud between after-watch and fo'castle drove the officers into an alliance of self-defense. A grave clash between the captain and the second mate seemed inevitable. It was a night of intolerable heat, and a sky spangled with stars hung over us low and smothering. Lawrence, the second mate, was off watch, and joined us, carrying a violin. Then under the weird depression and melancholy lassitude which burdened us all, he began to improvise. Mansfield and I listened, spell-bound. Under his touch the catgut gave off such strains as could come only from the sheer genius of a gifted musician who had suffered miserably. It was almost as if he were giving without words the story which his lips would never tell, and into the improvised music crept infinite pathos and somber tragedy. No one could have listened unmoved, but the manner in which Captain Coulter was affected was startling.

He came over with an advent like that of a maniac. The lame foot was pounding the deck with the stressful stamp that was always his indication of rage. He halted before us with fists clenched and his eyes glittering. Upon Lawrence he vented an outpouring of blasphemous and unquotable wrath.

"Throw that damned fiddle overboard," was the command with which he capped his fierce tirade. "Don't let me hear its hell-tortured screeching on my ship again."

For a moment Lawrence stood silent and cold in a petrifaction of anger. Then he laid the instrument carefully on a hatch and stepped forward. Obviously it was in his mind at that moment to kill the captain, but after a pause he thought better of it. The odds against him were too heavy.

"I'll stow the violin in my box, sir," he said with a voice so quiet it was almost gentle, "but so help me God, if ever we meet after this voyage is ended, I mean to kill you." Coulter laughed disdainfully and strode away, but for ten minutes Lawrence sat silent, his breath coming in deep gasps while he wrestled with the murder madness. We learned later that the captain was one of those persons whom music frenzies, and from that time on we did not even permit ourselves the consolation of whistling a favorite air.

Of all the restless men in the fo'castle, Coulter most keenly watched one John Hoak, a gigantic seaman from Liverpool, in whom he instinctively recognized a potential ringleader of mutiny. One evening Hoak vindicated this appraisement by defiantly and loudly playing a music-hall tune on an accordion. A strain of it reached the bridge and Coulter, who was on watch, ordered the offender forward. After a violent and profane denunciation, under which the giant writhed in silent fury, Coulter lashed out to the sailor's mouth with his clenched fist and sent him sprawling to the deck. But lest this conduct should appear too irresolute, he added the punishment of twenty-four hours in irons. A fellow seaman plucked up the heroism to demand that the incident be entered on the log for admiralty investigation and Coulter's only reply was to send the insurgent into the inferno of the stoke hold for an extra shift at the shovels. In the stokehold the thermometer registered 130 degrees Fahrenheit, and the white and brown torsos that strained under the trembling dials were black with the sooty sweat of their effort and red with the pitiless glare from the grates.

From these beginnings the cloud on the horizon of our affairs steadily gathered and blackened until an ominous pall of impending mutiny overhung us. Only an occasional coral reef or atoll now broke the monotony of a dead and oily sea. No shred of cloud relieved the emptiness of a devitalized sky. Mansfield and I went about in canvas shoes and pajamas. The ship was more disheveled than we, and its discipline more slovenly than its dress. The churlish silence of the fo'castle was met by the braggart autocracy of the officers. Conditions grew tenser and thicker with each day, yet no specific rupture came to fire the waiting explosion. Slowly it brewed and gathered menace, while the air hung pulseless and heavy under its shadow. Mansfield and I knew it needed only a lightning flash to loose all the artillery of the thunders and set them about their hell's fury. By tacit consent we did not often talk of it, but we remained close together and placed our revolvers, belts and sheath-knives where they could be readily caught up. Under the silent horror of foreboding our nerves became raw and our tempers, like those of the others, short and raspy. On one sultry afternoon when the trade wind was dead, I came upon Mansfield sprawling in the shadow of a life-boat, diligently reading entries from the unknown girl's diary, touching the incidents of her sheltered and untroubled life. He glanced up shamefacedly, then began in exculpation:

"See here, you know you're quite wrong about the guiltiness of reading this. I'm sure she wouldn't mind. She's not that sort. Here we are menaced by the inferno of a mutiny. We are no better than mice waiting the pleasure of a cat, which means to crush them.... The atmosphere will drive us mad. This book is like a breeze off the heather.... I tell you it helps."

In abnormal times men entertain abnormal ideas and warped notions. I sat cross-legged on the deck beside him and stuffed tobacco into my pipe. I said nothing.

"It's all getting on my nerves. I'm losing my grip!" he admitted. "Last night I dreamed of a nasty row and all day a bit of rhyme has been running through my brain." He paused a moment, then quoted:

"'Twas a cutlass swipe or an ounce of leadOr a yawning hole in a battered head,And the scuppers glut with a rotting red.

"'And there they lay while the soggy skiesDreened all day long in upstaring eyes,At murk sunset and at foul sunrise.'"

He broke off and laughed at himself unsteadily.

"Get your mind off it," I commanded shortly. "Fetch out the blank-book. Let's read about her début party."

But the passage at which the book fell open dealt with a time prior to débuts. At the head of the page was pasted a newspaper clipping hinting at personalities but giving no names.

"One of the most beautiful and popular members of the younger set in the summer colony" had been capsized while sailing in the harbor. The youth who accompanied her had been seized with cramps and she had kept not only herself but her helpless escort above water until the tardy arrival of help. Beneath, in her own hand, was scrawled:

"Did they expect me to drown him? I had to stand by, of course. What else could a fellow do? But I spoiled a dress I look nice in. I'm sorry for that."

Appended to this was a postscript so badly written that it was hard to decipher. I could guess that her cheeks had colored as she wrote it.

"Maybe after all, I am a grandstander. I did get awfully tired—and I pretended that *he* was looking on, and was swimming out to help me."

"By Jove" snorted Mansfield, "she's a ripping good sort. I wonder who she pretended was looking on."

"Turn back," I suggested. "It may tell."

But it was only after some searching that we found him duly catalogued, and even then she gave him no name. Yet in trailing him through the pages, we came to know her quite well, and to render sincere allegiance. She was not at all conventional. She was one of those rare discoveries upon which the prospector in life comes only when he strikes an El Dorado. She dared to think her own thoughts and did not grow into the stereotyped mold of imitation. We felt from the clean, instinctive courage of her tone and viewpoint that if ill chance had marooned her with us on this imperiled ship, she would bear herself more gallantly than we could hope to do, and that she would tread these filthy decks with no spots on the whiteness of her skirts.

In her early writings she had shown for something of a tomboy and there were hints of elderly exhortation to tread more primly the paths which were deemed maidenly. Yet from these tattered scraps of life and outlook, we could piece together some concept of her soul fabric. This girl was woven of pure silk, but not of flimsy silk; there were strength and softness— resoluteness and tenderness—a warp and woof for the loom of noble things—and charm. Often I felt as though I were invading a temple in which I had no place as communicant, and into whose fanes and outer areas I should wish to come reverently, with the shoes of my grosser soul in my hands. One night she had been sitting in the moonlight on the beach, and the sea had talked to her. What she wrote that night was pure poetry. I shall not try to reproduce it from my faulty memory. My heavy masculine hand would mar its gossamer beauty. One might as well undertake to restore the iridescent subtleties of a broken bubble. On this occasion she was thinking of the mysterious man she had so quaintly idealized. Had the lucky beggar, whoever he was, read those lines he must have felt that, in the lists of life, there rested on him the sacred obligation to bear a spotless shield and a true lance. She transcribed as one to whom the magic and delicate nuances of life are revealed. Besides these passages there were others sparkling with the merriment of spontaneous humor. Our writer was no Lady Dolorosa. She was as many-sided and many-hued as the diamond whose facets break light into color. She frankly admitted to these pages, intended only for herself, that she was beautiful, though she wished that her eyes were blue instead of gray-brown, and that her type were different. Evidently she had cut her teeth on compliment and fed from childhood on that type of admiration which beauty exacts. She seemed to be a little hungry for tributes of a different and deeper sort. In her society days, as in the more youthful period, we found frequent references to the unnamed man who still held his undeserved and paramount place as an idealized personality; a human touchstone by which she tested the intrinsicness of other men—always to the detriment of those on trial.

---

# CHAPTER V

## PREMONITIONS BECOME REALITIES

At last, running back to the start, we tracked him down and with his discovery came disappointment. I had realized that she had been dressing a mere lay-figure in garments of idealized manhood and endowing an unknown with a panoply of the chivalric to which he could probably lay no rightful claim. Still it was disconcerting to realize that he had, in the flesh, contributed absolutely nothing to the picture. She had simply devised from the whole cloth of imagination a collaborative sum of Galahad the Pure and Richard the Lion-Hearted. She had seen him only once in later years—from the sidelines of a Yale-Harvard football game. He was playing with the crimson and she was at the impressionable age. There was the whole and meager foundation for his apotheosis. She did not state the year, but she gave the score, and by that I identified the occasion.

"I devoutly pray," I confided to young Mansfield, "that she never meets him. She has fed herself on dreams. I hope she doesn't wake up."

Mansfield promptly took up the unknown hero's defense. He invariably held a brief for the idealist.

"Why do you assume that he's a bounder?" he demanded almost resentfully. "He may be all she thinks."

"I don't assume anything," I retorted, "but I happened to play on that team myself and I am compelled to admit, though with chagrin, that we had among us no knights from Arthur's Round Table. Warriors of ferocity we had; young gentlemen who played the game to the lasting glory of John Harvard; but this letter-perfect type of chivalry, valor and gentleness well, I'm afraid he failed to make the team."

You remember the story of Bruce and the spider? In his ermine, surrounded by his stalwart barons, Robert would probably have learned no lesson from the weaving of filmy webs. Alone and in peril, it taught him how to conquer. To us, alone and in peril, this diary assumed an epochal importance entirely out of kelter with its face value.

Of course, there were many topics which we might have discussed to divert our minds from morbidly watching the cloud of impending mutiny spread and grow inky. But the cloud was present and human, and the diary was present and human, and we were present and human. Whether or not we were creatures of atrophied brains and distorted vision is an academic question. The fact remains. For us there was genuine relief in turning from the miasma of brooding doom which overhung the *Wastrel* to the spiced fragrance of this self-revealed personality. It was a clean breeze into our asphyxiation. It was a momentary excursion out of a noisome dungeon into an old-fashioned garden, where roses nod and illusions bloom.

One steaming night when darkness had stopped our reading, the two of us were lying flat on our backs—and silent—in the enveloping shadows of the forward deck near the capstan. A group of men who were off watch had gathered near us, seeking the gratefulness of the uninterrupted breeze. With no suspicion of our proximity, they fell into a low-pitched but violent conference.

Hoak held the floor as spokesman, and his deep whispering voice was raw with bitterness.

"We hain't no bloomin' galley-slyves," he growled. "Blyme me, I say, let's make a hend o' the 'ole bloody mess once and for hall."

"How?" came the natural question from one of the more conservative.

"'Ow?" retorted the ringleader, "W'at's the odds 'ow? Any way will do. Rush the cabin. There's a stand of rifles at the for'ard bulkhead. Kill hoff the bloody lot of hofficers. Navigate the bloomin' ole 'ooker back ourselves and report whatever damn thing we like."

"How about these passengers? They'd snitch," suggested the same questioner.

"Aw no," sarcastically assured Hoak, "they won't snitch. They won't 'ave no more charnce to snitch than Coulter 'isself—damn 'im."

For a moment I felt a steaming throb in my throat. Then came a new sensation, something like relief that at last the clear outline was looming through the fog of maddening uncertainty. It did not seem to matter so much what the certainty was, so long as it brought an end to the suspense. There was some discussion in hushed voices. Caution had its advocates who opposed so desperate a course.

"Think it hover till to-morrow," said Hoak at last. "But hif you don't stand by me Hi'm going to cut loose a boat and tyke to the water. To 'ell with the *Wastrel* an' her rotter of a captain."

There was a sudden hush followed by a sort of low chorused groan. Around the superstructure of the forward cabin appeared Captain Coulter, his first officer and the chief engineer. For an instant they stood silently, flashing electric torches into the terrified faces of the conspirators who, like schoolboys caught denouncing their teacher, shuffled their feet and remained speechless.

Hoak, alone, took a step forward. His face was working spasmodically in the bull's-eye glare which exaggerated the high lights on his snarling teeth and the black shadows of his scowl. He wavered for an instant between his personal dread of Coulter, and the knowledge that, with so much already known, caution was futile. While he hesitated the other men tacitly grouped themselves together at his back and stood sullenly eying the officers. Coulter and his two subordinates slipped their hands into their pockets. It was a tense moment and a noiseless one. When the captain broke silence his voice was cool, almost casual.

"Mr. Kirkenhead," he ordered the chief engineer, "take this man Hoak to the stokehold, and keep him there until we reach port. Give him double shift and if he makes a false move—kill him."

The giant made a passionate start forward, and found himself looking down the barrel of Coulter's magazine pistol. From the glint of the raised weapon he bounced backward against the rail, where he leaned incoherently snarling like a cornered dog.

"Hi didn't sign as no blymed stoker," he growled at last. "Hi won't go———"

"The stokehold or hell, it's up to you." Coulter's reply came in an absolute monotony of voice strangely at variance with the passionate stress of their labored breathing. Back of the tableau gleamed the phosphorescence of the placid sea. "There's thirty seconds to decide. Mr. Kirkenhead, look at your watch."

For a seeming eternity there was waiting and bated breath. We could hear the muffled throb of the engines, and the churning of the screws.

Then Kirkenhead announced, "Twenty seconds, sir."

A moment more and Hoak turned, dropping his head in utter dejection and shambled aft toward the engine-room companionway.

"Mr. Heffernan," came the captain's staccato orders, "instruct the ship's carpenter to scuttle all the boats, except the port and starboard ones on the bridge. If we are to have any little disagreements on board we will settle them among ourselves. No one will leave in my boats except by my orders. And"—he wheeled on the men—"whenever you vermin feel inclined for trouble—start it."

So that incident passed and went to swell the cumulative poison of festering hatred. We knew that the eruption had merely been delayed; that it must inevitably come and that now its coming would be soon. Between forward and aft war had been declared. Later that same evening I made bold to remonstrate with Captain Coulter as to the order concerning the boats. The conversation took place on the bridge—and it was brief.

"Mr. Mansfield and myself," I said, "are passengers who have paid full fares and we are entitled to full rights. We demand protection. This hulk is rotten and unseaworthy. When you scuttle her boats you are throwing the parachute out of a leaky balloon."

Coulter looked me over for a moment and replied with absolute composure.

"Mr. Deprayne, rights are good things—when you can enforce them. Consulates and courts of admiralty are a long way off. The intervening water is quite deep. If you don't like the *Wastrel*, leave it. I'm sorry I can't spare you a boat to leave in."

Mansfield and myself went that night in the miserable cabin which we shared oppressed with the conviction that the breaking point was at hand. Mansfield had suddenly sloughed off his boyishness and become unexpectedly self-contained, giving the impression of capability. The prospect of action had changed him. Once more he began to quote his ghastly verses, but now without shuddering, almost cheerfully.

"'Twas a cutlass swipe or an ounce of lead,Or a yawning hole in a battered head—And the scuppers glut with a rotting red.'"

Then he remembered that sometimes men survive strange adventures, and he wrote a letter to the girl in Sussex which he asked me to deliver in the event that I, and not he, should prove such a survivor. I fastened it with a pin into the pocket of my pajama jacket. For hours after we had turned into our berths each of us knew that the other was not sleeping. We heard the crazy droning of the sick engine; the wash of the quiet water; the straining of the timbers.

We had not, on turning in, followed our usual custom of blowing out the vile-smelling oil lamp which gave our stateroom its only illumination. Neither of us had spoken of it, but we left the light burning probably in tacit presentiment that this was to be a night of some portentous development, and one not to be spent in darkness. Mansfield pretended to sleep in the upper berth, but after vainly courting dreams for an hour, I slipped out of mine and crept to the fresher air of the deck.

When I returned to the cabin, still obsessed with restless wakefulness, I found the diary, and throwing myself into my bunk, spent still another hour in its perusal. I had long ago laid by my early scruples and now I found in its pages a quality strangely soothing.

Singularly enough, in all our fragmentary reading between these limp covers, we had never pursued any consecutive course and though certain passages had been re-read until I fancy both of us could have quoted them from memory, there still remained others upon which we had not touched. For me in my present condition of jumping nerves they offered fields of quieting exploration. Now, for a time, I skipped about, reading here and there passages in no way connected. There was a highly humorous description of a certain Frenchman who had insistently shadowed the course of the girl's travels about the Continent, inflicting on her an homage which it seemed to me must have been more offensive than actual rudeness. She did not give his name, but her description of his appearance and eccentricities was so droll and keenly appreciative that even my strained lips curled into a grin of enjoyment in the perusal. He had a coronet to bestow and she likened his attitude and bearing to that of a crested cock robin. "To-night," she wrote, "*monsieur le comte* proposed for my hand—to Mother. I was in the next room and heard it. To hear one's self proposed to by proxy is quite the most amusing thing that can happen. When he asks me I shall inform him that I've already given my heart to another man—a man who hasn't asked me and may never ask me. Yes, he will, too. He *must*. It is in my horoscope. 'The Heavens rolled between us at the end, we shall but vow the faster for the stars.' This little Frenchman needs an heiress and it might as well be me—but it won't be."

This was the first intimation that the unknown author of these pages was possessed of wealth as well as beauty. In a vague way I found myself regretting the discovery, although I could not say why. Through these pages breathed the distinction of a piquant and subtly charming personality—the fact that she had fortune as well, could add nothing. But as I read the paragraphs devoted to her odyssey across the continent and around the borders of the Mediterranean, shadowed always by this persistent suitor with his picayune title, it struck me that her itinerary and the order of her going tallied with my own wanderings. Yet that might have no significance, since the routes of European touring are distressingly devoid of variation.

The finger of destiny had seemed to concern itself in the fashion in which I had always just missed the lady of Naples, Monte Carlo and Cairo by a margin of seconds and of untoward circumstance. If my Fate were playing with me in this manner it appeared consistent with its policy of tantalizing evasiveness that she and the writer might be the same. When I had given up the pursuit and come away to this remote quarter of the globe it might still be decreed that I should not escape her influence.

Having skipped about for a time in such haphazard fashion, the idea seized me of going back to the beginning and reading from the commencement down to the present.

In the first pages of course I encountered a certain immature crudity of composition and yet, in spite of these things, there was much here of the charming fascination of childhood and the beginnings of character. If the later sections were as fragrant as flowers, the earlier passages were like the annals of rosebuds and blossoms. I believe I have already mentioned that in her childhood she had been something of a tomboy. Her interests had seemed to include many things which might quite naturally have belonged to the enthusiasms of her brothers. Also one read between the lines that her charming sense of humor and self-containment had developed upon overcome tendencies toward passionate temper. A certain passage had to do with her experience at a girls' boarding-school when she was probably not more than ten or eleven. One of the teachers—an unimpeachable lady of great learning and little human perception, it would seem—had aroused her intense disfavor. There were various references to this feud and also, even so early, to the mysterious person vaguely alluded to as He. The principal of the school harbored a bull terrier of rather uncertain temper. This brute, save for total fealty to his mistress and to the writer of the diary, seemed to hold in his nature only distrust for humanity, and among those specially singled out for his antipathy was the aforementioned teacher.

One day the writer and the dog had met the preceptress on the avenue. The girl had set down with great glee, the terror with which her enemy had appealed to her for protection against the onslaughts of the dreaded Cerberus.

"I told her that I would hold him," naively related the entry, in a sprawling, childish hand, "and I did hold him until she was *almost* at the gate—but when I let him go I gave him a little sound advice and he took it."

There followed a vivid description, done into mirth-provoking humor, of the somewhat strenuous events of the next twenty or thirty seconds. A section of black alpaca skirt remained with the dog as a memento.

"Of course," commented the writer, "I couldn't laugh freely until I got back to the house, but I am laughing now. She looked so absurd! As I came in I saw Him ride by on horseback. I'm afraid he wouldn't approve."

The description of that teacher had reminded me strongly of my good Aunt Sarah. The explanation that the dog had been the child's friend merely because she had refused to be afraid, was so convincingly put that I found myself in guilty accord with her point of view. In a dozen ways, despite this single instance, she showed that her pity and tenderness were very genuine and sensitive, and easily reached by any true appeal.

This going back to the beginning enabled me to meet, on the occasion of his first appearance, the man who had exercised such a strong influence upon her subsequent life. In this I was pleased, for it showed that however imaginary may have been his aura of ideality, none the less it had basis in something more substantial than a glimpse of a football game. There was, too, an element touching and almost pathetic in this earliest self-confessed love. He was when she first saw him, eighteen or nineteen, and she half as old. This disparity in age had put a chasm between them which it did not occur to her that the years would bridge. He was just at that self-sufficient age, when he regarded himself as very much a man and short-skirted, pigtailed females as very far beneath his mature devotion. Yet, in his patronizing way, he had been decently kind and had jeopardized his standing as a man-of-the-world by impersonal courtesies to a little girl. His influence had accordingly grown strong and permanent, though he had not known of its existence. She had enviously watched him with girls a few years her senior and had admired his frank, sportsmanlike attitude and freedom from callow freshness—and his courage. She said quite frankly in the diary that she did not suppose he had remembered her at all.

And so, as I lay sleepless and oppressed by presentiment of disaster, I read from childhood to young womanhood her chronicle of ideals until, under the soothing of the document, I at last fell into a doze.

# CHAPTER VI

## THE END OF THE "WASTREL"

When sleep came to me it was fitful with a thousand nightmare impossibilities, I saw, in my dreams, the face of the stale sea and sky translated into a broad human visage paralyzed and smiling unendingly in that hideous grin which stamps the tortured teeth of the lockjaw victim. Then the monster of the dream broke out of its fixity and with a shriek of hurricanes aimed a terrific blow at the prow of the *Wastrel*. The ship shivered, trembled and collapsed. With a stifled gasp I woke. Our sickly lantern was guttering in a sooty stream of smoke. Young Mansfield stood in the center of the cabin buckling his pistol belt. From somewhere came a sound of rushing water and a medley of shouts and oaths and pistol shots. A dingy rat scuttled wildly out from between my feet and whisked away through the crack under our bolted door. While I stood there stupidly inactive, hardly as yet untangling fact and dream, Mansfield handed me my belt and revolver.

"Slip on your shoes and fetch along a life-belt," he commanded steadily. "It has come."

We jerked open the door and groped along the alley-way in darkness, and, as we guided our steps with hands fumbling the walls, water washed about our ankles. The lights there had gone out. With one guiding hand on the wall and one on Mansfield's shoulder, I made my labored way toward the deck ladder.

Without a word and as of right, the young Englishman, who had heretofore lacked initiative, now assumed command of our affairs. We needed no explanation to tell us that the pandemonium which reigned above was not merely the result of mutiny. A hundred patent things testified that this shambling tramp of the seas had received a mortal hurt. The stench of bilge sickened us as the rising water in her hull forced up the heavy and fetid gases. The walls themselves were aslant under a dizzy careening to starboard.

She must have steamed full front on to a submerged reef and destruction. It was palpably no matter of an opening seam. She had been torn and ripped in her vitals. She was dying fast and in inanimate agony. In the rickety engine-room something had burst loose under the strain. Now as she sank and reeled there came a hissing of steam; a gasping, coughing, hammering convulsion of pistons, rods and driving shafts, suddenly turned into a junk heap running amuck.

It is questionable whether there would have been time to lower away boats had the most perfect discipline and heroism prevailed. There was no discipline. There were no available boats, except the two hanging from the bridge davits, and about them, as we stumbled out on the decks, raged a fierce battle of extermination, as men, relapsed to brutes, fought for survival.

I have since that night often and vainly attempted to go back over that holocaust and arrange its details in some sort of chronology. I saw such ferocity and confusion, turning the deck into a shambles in an inconceivably short space, that even now I cannot say in what sequence these things happened. I have a jumbled picture in which certain unimportant details stand out distinctly while great things are vague. I can still see, in steel-black relief, the silhouetted superstructure, funnels and stanchions; the indigo shadows and ghostly spots of white under a low-swinging half-moon and large softly-glowing stars. The sky was clear and smiling, in the *risor sardonicus* of my dream.

I have sometimes felt that all the difference between the courageous and craven lies in the chance of the instant with which the numbers fall on the dice of life. To-day's coward may be to-morrow's hero. For an instant, with an unspeakable babel in my ears and a picture of human battle in my eyes, I knew only the chaotic confusion that comes of panic. Then I caught a glimpse of one detail and all physical fear fell away from me. I found myself conscious only of contempt for the struggling, clawing terror of these men who were as reasonless and ineffective as stampeding cattle. The detail which steadied me like a cold shower was the calmness of young Mansfield as he waited at my side, his face as impersonally puzzled as though he were studying in some museum cabinet a new and strange specimen of anthropological interest.

We both stood in the shadow of the forward superstructure as yet unseen. All the ferocity of final crisis swirled and eddied about the bridge upon which we looked as men in orchestra chairs might look across the footlights on a stage set for melodrama. Apparently the crew had already discovered to its own despair that Coulter's inhuman orders for scuttling the boats had been carried out, and that of all the emergency craft carried by the *Wastrel*, only those ridiculously insufficient ones hanging by the port and starboard lights of the bridge offered a chance of escape. At all events, the other boats hung neglected and unmanned. That the whole question was one of minutes was an unescapable conclusion. One could almost feel the settling of the crazy, ruptured hull as the moments passed and each time I turned my head to glance back with a fascinated impulse at the smoke-stack I could see that its line tilted further from the vertical.

Heffernan was in charge of the starboard boat, already beginning to run down its lines, and over that on the port side, Coulter himself held command.

It seemed that when the moment of final issue came, a few of the foremast men had preferred entrusting their chances to obeying the captain, whose effectiveness had been proven, to casting their lots with their mates. These were busy at the tackle. On the deck level howled and fought the mutineers. Already corpses were cluttering the space at the foot of the steep ladder that gave—and denied—access to the bridge. Probably the revolver shots we had heard as we groped our way from our cabin had been the chief officer's terse response to the first mad rush for that stairway. Now as he awaited the lowering away, Coulter stood above, looking down on the sickening confusion with a grim expression which was almost amusement. The fighting went on below where the frantic, terror-stricken fellows swarmed and grappled and swayed and disabled each other in the effort to gain the ladder. But when someone rose out of the maelstrom and struggled upward it was only to be knocked back by the ax, upon which, in the brief intervals between assaults, Coulter leaned contemplating the battle-royal. The revolver he had put back in his pocket. It was not needed, and he was conserving its effectiveness for another moment.

In telling it, the picture seems clear enough, but in the seeing, it was a thing of horrible and tangled details, enacted as swiftly as a moving-picture film run too rapidly on its reel.

There were shouts and quick staccato orders piercing the blending of terrorized voices—an oath snapped out—a shriek—a struggling mass—a desperate run up the ladder—hands straining aloft to pull down the climber and clear the way—a swift blow from above, a thud on the deck below—a sickening vision of slaughter. Over it all pounded the hammering racket from the disorganized engines. Soon came the stench of smoke and out of one of the after hatches mounted a thin tongue of orange flame, snapping and sputtering vengefully for a moment, then leaping up with a suddenly augmented roar. The twin elements of destruction, water and fire, were vying in the work of annihilation.

I turned my head for an instant to look back at the new menace, and clutched Mansfield's arm. Aloof with folded arms against the rail, making no effort to participate in the riot, stood young Lawrence. The fast-spreading flames lit up his face. His attitude and expression were those of quiet disgust. His lips were set in scorn for the superlative excitement of his fellows. He was the stoic awaiting the end, with a smile of welcome for the acid test which held, for him, no fear. It was as though the rising rim of water brought a promise of grateful rest. He saw ahead nothing except release from all the wild turmoil and misery which had spoken itself without words that evening when Coulter had silenced the improvisation of his violin.

But if the end was a thing of quiet philosophy to Lawrence, it was not so to others. The lurid flare, which turned the impassioned picture in a moment from a silhouette of blacks and cobalts to a crimson hell, seemed to inflame to greater madness men already mad. There was a rush for the rails. We saw figures leaping into the sea. There had been some hitch on the bridge, due no doubt to the miserable condition of everything aboard the disheveled tramp. The boats were not yet launched, but now the men were embarking. Coulter himself was the last to leap for the swinging boat, and a moment before he did so Hoak appeared. He had miraculously made his way alive out of the engine-room's inferno, and his coming was that of a maniac. His huge body, bare to the waist, sweat-streaked and soot-blackened and fire-blistered, was also dark with blood. His voice was raised in demented laughter and every vestige of reason had deserted eyes that were now agleam only with homicidal mania. From the companionway to the bridge, his course was as swift and sure as a homing pigeon's. He brandished the shovel with which he had been shamefully forced to feed the maws of the furnaces. The struggling men fell back before his onslaught. But Hoak had no care for self-preservation. His sole mission was reprisal.

The fight about the ladder's foot had waned. With a leap that carried him half-way up and an agility that knew no thwarting the madman made the upper level. The tyrannical despot of the vessel, standing poised for his swing to the boat raised the pistol which had already halted other mad rushes during the last sanguinary minutes. At its bark Hoak staggered to his knees, but was up again and charging forward with the impetus of a wounded rhinoceros. He had one deed to do before he died and would not be denied. The flying shovel narrowly missed the captain's head as he jumped for the boat, but the seaman with his lips parted over the snarl of clenched teeth fought his painful way to the davit, gripping a knife which he had brought in his belt. His eyes glowed with the strange light that madness lends and his muscles were tensed in the brief exaggerated strength of a supreme effort. He hurled himself to the out-swung support and seizing the stern line began hacking at its tarred tautness as he bellowed ghastly laughter and blasphemies. Coulter from his place below sent two more bullets into the great hulk of flesh that hung tenaciously and menacingly above him, but, as the second spat out, the rope, none too good at best, parted and the boat, held only by its bow line, swung down with a mighty snap, spilling its occupants into the sea like apples tossed from an overturned plate. We had a momentary glimpse of the captain clinging to the gunwale, his legs lashing out flail-like. Then his hold loosened and he fell with a splash into the phosphorus water where the sharks were already gathering. And at the same moment, his mission performed, Hoak slowly slid around the curving davit and dropped limply after him.

Young Mansfield's voice came vaguely to my ear. "They've overlooked the life-raft," he said. "Let's have a try at that. There's not much time now."

The starboard scuppers were letting in sea water and the flames were creeping close, as we turned together, holding to the shadows of the superstructure, and ran forward.

We were tearing our fingers raw over stiffened knots when a rush of feet interrupted us. The next instant I saw my companion lashing out with the butt of his pistol, and surrounded by a quartette of assailants. In the moonlight he loomed gigantic and heroic of proportion. I, too, was surrounded and conscious only of a wild new elation and battle-lust, as I fought.

Suddenly there came a terrific shock, preceded by a wildly screaming hiss in the bowels of the *Wastrel's* hull. The torn shell quivered in an insensate death-rattle, and under a detonation at once hollow and loud a mass of timbers shot upward amidships. The boilers had let go and we hung wavering for the final plunge, yet it did not come at once. Then I suppose I was struck by falling débris. With a dizzy sense of stars dancing as lawlessly as rocket sparks and dying as quickly into blackness, I lost all hold on consciousness.

---

# CHAPTER VII

## IN STRANGE CIRCUMSTANCES.

Pongee pajamas and a revolver belt constitute a light equipment even for the tropics, but that was the least pressing of my concerns.

How long I had remained insensible I can only estimate, but often there come back to me, from that time, wraith-like shreds of memory in which I seem to have drifted down the centuries. I recall for one thing a stunned and throbbing aching back of the eyes and a half-conscious gazing up at rocking stars.

At all events, when rational understanding returned to me, the sun was glaring insufferably from a scorched zenith. I began to patch together fragments of memory and to call loudly for Mansfield. There was no answer, and when I attempted to rise I found myself roughly lashed to the life-raft by several turns of a line so tightly drawn that the sensory nerves in my legs gave no response to my movements.

My support was rocking in its lodgment between two weed-trailing boulders, stained like verdigris and licked smooth by the lapping of the sea. Off to my front stretched waters, so quiet that they seemed almost tideless, though at a distance I could hear the running of surf. To look behind involved a painful twisting of my neck, but I made the effort, and was rewarded with the sight of land. A quarter of a mile away smooth reaches of white sand met the water in a graciously inviting beach. Beyond it and mounting upward from palm fringe to snow-cap rose the very respectable proportions of a volcanic island. The coral rocks which had caught my raft were outposts of many others that went trooping shoreward, breaking, here and there, the surface of jade-green shallows.

From the deep turquoise of the outer sea to the white rim of the sands ran a gamut of colorful beauty. The mountain, as symmetrically coned as Fuji-yama, stood over it all in grave dominance. Off to the left sponge-like cliffs broke steeply upward from the level of the beach and about their clefts circled endless flights of gulls. There I knew the rising tide would thunder and break itself to pieces in a thousand plumes of spray.

But how had I reached this place and what had become of Mansfield? It must have been he who had lashed me to the raft. From no one else on the *Wastrel* could I have expected better treatment than "a cutlass swipe or an ounce of lead." Palpably, he had emerged from the battle victor, and, save for myself, sole survivor. I conjectured that when he had floated the raft from the partly submerged deck, he had found the spark of life still lurking in my pulses and had made me fast upon its timbers. Perhaps an over-trust in his ability to remain afloat had made him less careful of himself. Possibly he had lost consciousness as we drifted and had been washed over-side, to fall prey to the prowling sharks. I could not hope to know what his end had been, but I wished that I might have shared it with him.

I fumbled at the soaked knots of my rope with fingers that had grown numb. When, at last, I was free and had to some extent restored the circulation in my stagnant veins, I began the task of freeing my oarless craft from its wedged position so that the insetting tide might carry me to the shore.

In the pocket of my pajama jacket, soaked with salt water and almost reduced to a pulp, I found the letter which I stood charged to deliver to the girl in Sussex. I laughed. I knew that I was not in reality the solitary survivor of the *Wastrel*. I was merely the latest survivor. I was to die more slowly than my fellows. This sun, at the end of my lingering, would beat down on my bones, whitened, disjointed and perhaps vulture-plucked. The revolver in my belt was already clouding into red rust under the washing of the night's salt water. I experimentally turned the cylinder and found that the corrosion had not yet attacked the mechanism. One cartridge could cheat my sentence of slow death, yet I did not fire the shot.

Life had heretofore been a thing I would have willingly surrendered. Now, I found myself standing precariously on the narrow and very slippery edge of existence, and with Death advancing on me I no longer wished to die. The very odds against me brought a dogged desire to cling until my feet should slip and my fingers could no longer hold their life-grip. Meantime I should probably go mad, but that lay hereafter. At present I had only to wait for the tide. Since I could not hurry the ocean pulse, I must lie there thinking.

From the sea I could look for rescue only by a miracle. What had been Coulter's course or destination he had not confided, but I knew that we had for days been in imperfectly charted waters where our screws had perhaps kicked up a virgin wake. We had passed atolls marked, on the chart, P. D. and even E. D. ("position doubtful" and "existence doubtful"), and to hope that some other wanderer might shortly follow would be taxing coincidence too far.

Only God knew what type of human, animal and reptilian life the island held. I could view it across the accursedly beautiful waterway and speculate upon its nature, but I could beat up no confidence in its treatment of me. Its aspect would have been magnificent had its lush greenery not wrapped and softened every commanding crag and angle, but it was a loveliness which suggested treacherous menace; the deceptive beauty of the panther or of the soft-gliding snake that charms its prey to death.

Isolation here would sap my mental essence and atrophy my brain, unless some device could be found by which I could side-focus and divert my trend of thought. Even had the young girl's diary remained to me, I might by it have kept myself reminded of life in those civilized spots which I could hardly hope to revisit; and so I might die sane. A single book would have helped. I had been credited with a sense of the ludicrous so whimsical as to be almost irresponsible. If now I could invoke that facetious quality to my salvation I might hope to be regarded as a consistent humorist.

At length I saw that the tide was setting in, carrying my raft with it, and realized that I was hungry. When I had once more under my feet the feel of solid earth, the sun was hanging near the snow-capped crater of the volcano. I left for to-morrow all problems of exploration, and stripping to the skin, ran up and down the soft sand of the beach until the blood was once more pulsing regularly through my naked body. Then on hands and knees I pursued and devoured numbers of the unpalatable crabs that scuttled to hiding under slimy tangles of sea weed. My throat was hot and sticky with the parch of thirst, but as night fell the jungle began to loom darkly, a forbidding hinterland, and no fresh water came down to my beach.

The melting snow was a guarantee of springs and a man can endure three days without drinking if he must. I stretched myself between two large rocks just upward of the high-tide line, cursing stout Cortez and all those perniciously active souls who insisted on discovering the Pacific Ocean.

Sleep did not at once come to my relief. I saw the stars, close and lustrous, parade across the night, and instead of planning while I lay awake practical things for the morrow, as a good woodsman might have done, I was thinking futilely of the psychological features of my predicament. Possibly the doctor's prediction of insanity had lain dormant in some brain cell from which it was now emerging to frighten me. I feared less for the hunger of my body than for the impossibility of feeding my mind. It occurred to me that keeping a record of my emotions would at once serve to fight back atrophy and leave an interesting record for those who might, but almost certainly would not, come in after days to the island. Then I recalled that in my penless and paperless plight I was as far from the possibility of writing as from the power to ring for a taxicab and drive home.

Yet the idea of a diary fascinated me. I wished to write in frankness what it felt like to die at the foot of an undiscovered volcano. There came to my mind an example I wished to emulate. I had come upon a report made public by the Naval Department of Japan in which was quoted a letter written by Lieutenant Sakuma, from the bottom of Hiroshima Bay, where his submarine had struck and failed to rise again.

Most of his crew lay dead in the sunken vessel, and he himself was slowly and painfully succumbing to strangulation. He devoted to a note of apology addressed to his Emperor those hours spent in dying, and expressed the hope that his message might, in future, be of value in the avoidance of similar fatalities. He praised the gallantry of his subordinates.

The letter, read in the Mikado's palace a week later, when the submarine had been raised with its dead, was in the stoic style of the race and severely official. It culminated in a broken sentence.

"It is now 12:30 P. M. My breathing is so difficult and painful—I thought I could blow out gasoline but I am intoxicated with it—Captain Nakano—it is now 12:40 P. M.—I——"

There it ended. It seemed to me that if I could busy myself in faint duplicate, with so human a record of approaching the ferry, I could be in a measure consoled. Then gazing at the Southern Cross, before sleep brought respite, I found myself thinking once more of the elusive lady who had so often escaped my inquisitive glance and whose face I should now never see.

---

# CHAPTER VIII

## NATURE INDULGES IN SATIRE

Though I am not giving authorship to this narrative with a view to its general perusal, I am determined so to write it that if other eyes do chance upon it they may read the true records of a man's emotions under those circumstances.

I shall never be able to coax myself into any illusion of heroism in my adventures and I shall set down my most abject terrors in equal and impartial degree with the few occasions in which the instinct of self-preservation enabled me to rise to the need and bluff magnificently.

The case of the submarine commander of Nippon was different. He wished to leave behind him such a message as an Emperor might read, and with exalted devotion to his object, he left it. Still, had some miracle brought his vessel to the surface before the end, who knows but that, in the confessional of his own memory, he might have acknowledged a very delirium of terror? Who knows but that between the period of one unflinching paragraph and the capital of the next, there may have been intervals of wallowing in the trough of physical despair?

At least with me there were many fears. The night went by a road of nightmare and thirst which led to no haven of rest. I slept fitfully and in terror, and awoke at its end to a feeling of exhaustion. For a while I dreaded to rise and face the possibilities of a new day. It was only the burning torture of thirst that finally outweighed panic and drove me in search of water. I held timidly to the shore, distrusting the jungle and dodging furtively from rock to rock, with straining eyes and ears. Climbing among the ragged boulders which were strewn like fragments of fallen masonry at the foot of the cliff, I shortly came upon a thread of clear water, where I lay and slaked my thirst. After that came a renewed freshness and a sudden return of vigor. I began also to feel a healthful hunger, and when, in clambering to the top of a steep rock, I frightened a shrieking gull from her nest, I fell avidly on the eggs she left behind.

As the sun climbed, a tepid humidity freighted the air, but the trade-wind, rising steadily and freshly, tempered it and stirred the delicate fronds of palm and fern.

The cliff was honeycombed with small irregular caverns and rifts. Some were mere grottoes, but others went back into somber recesses deeper than

I, with no means of lighting my steps, cared to explore. For my dwelling place I selected one that broadened from a twisted and narrow fissure to a crude chamber large enough for a wolf's den, or at need a man's refuge. A fern-fringed brooklet trickled across the opening.

For my door yard I had a small plateau with a sheer wall of cliff at my back and a steep drop at the front. One must climb to reach the place which is an advantage where the tenant may desire to roll stones down upon the heads of his visitors.

The *Wastrel* must have gone to the bottom near by, for incoming tides from time to time deposited on my shore strange and satirical scraps of flotsam. The sardonic humor of the sea mocked me by delivering on my beach a tattered fragment of old newspaper and an empty biscuit tin.

It was two days after my arrival that I discovered some bulky thing lodged, as my raft had been, upon the near-by rocks. The two days had told upon me. My pajamas were in ribbons; my canvas shoes torn, and my flesh bruised. My feet, too, were cut and blistered and my hands raw. I had already tired of talking aloud to myself and more and more often I caught myself turning with a sudden start to peer apprehensively at the fringe of the forest. To my growing morbidness it seemed that over the beauty of the place hung an impalpable but certain curse. I waded out eagerly to the fresh bit of salvage and found a seaman's chest with quaintly knotted handles of tarred rope. It was of stout workmanship and its heavy locks and hinges had endured without injury the buffeting of the sea. The name of J. H. Lawrence still legible upon one end brought back with startling vividness the memory of a man waiting with stoical amusement the coming of death. Laboriously enough I dragged it in, halting often to pant and wipe the sweat out of my eyes with my forearm.

The sun was sinking over the shoulder of the mountain when I at last arrived, exhausted but still tugging at my prize, upon the plateau of my cliff apartment. I lay a long while, my heart pounding with exertion, before I was equal to the task of attacking its lock with a stone and my sheath knife, and after that it was some moments before the lock yielded and I raised the heavy lid. First there met my eyes a scattered collection of souvenir postcards, much discolored and faded, but sufficiently preserved to awaken a clamor of protest and longing. There were tantalizing pictures of the Café de Paris and Trafalgar Square and the *bund* at Hong Kong.

Young Mr. Lawrence must have been a confirmed souvenir-buyer. I could trace his odyssey by trivial things he had picked up here and there. Two curved daggers with turquoise settings in the hilt had come from the bazaars of Damascus or Jerusalem. A copper incense-burner with a package of scented tapers had been brought from Tokio or Nagasaki. Equally useless things filled package after package.

No mission chest piously outfitted at home ever carried to the remote heathen a more useless assortment of unnecessaries than this one brought to me. There was not a shirt, not an article of utility, only trinkets as serviceable as doll-babies to a prizefighter. At last, however, I came upon two packages carefully wrapped in sail-cloth. So painstaking and secure had been their packing that when I took off the first covering and the second, I found that the contents had suffered no wetting.

The first bundle contained the violin which had incensed the captain and several packages of extra strings. As I took it out, I seemed to hear again its plaintive, wordless song and I laid it down reverently. It seemed a part of the dead man's soul—something intimate and wonderful which had outlasted his mortality.

In the second package was something wrapped in tissue paper and very soft to the touch. I opened it and spread out on the sand a gorgeously wrought Mandarin kimono. Its silk was of the heaviest and richest quality and its design flamed with the unstinted opulence of Chinese embroidery. On the flowing sleeves and bordered panels were storks of blue and silver flying among poppy-like flowers of crimson purple. There were also delicately worked streams and reeds and moons, all tangled up with ranting dragons of gold, gazing fiercely out from eyes of inset jade. Gold thread, silver thread, silk thread, cunningly combined to the making of its dazzling pattern.

Some celestial dignitary had once ordered its embroidering and, perhaps, had ridden upon his palanquin garbed in its splendor with the pride of a peacock in his narrow, slanting eyes. It seemed to me, kneeling there in my torn pajamas, my knees and elbows bruised, my stomach rebelling against rank food, that I could see the whole picture of which this garment had once been a brilliant detail. There were shouting coolies running ahead with huge bamboo staves to clear the way. The grandee's chair, crusted with carving, was borne along in state. I could picture paper lanterns swinging from slender poles and plum blossoms awave and smell the heavy reek of burning incense, and at the thought of all this arrogant luxury I suffered as though I were struggling through a nightmare. The young derelict of the *Wastrel* had, in all likelihood, bargained for it and haggled over its cost in an Oriental shop. He had finally bought it for a gift to a wife or sweetheart, and even with capable bargaining it must have been a purchase beyond his means. Now in futile magnificence it lay outspread before me who was sea-wrecked and fighting hunger. In the same package, however, I found my first useful articles: a small block of those miniature matches that one may buy in the Chinatown sections of San Francisco or New York, which burn with an odious reek of sulphur. It was doubtless because they partook of the quality of a curiosity that he had preserved them.

There was also one of those slung-shots such as may be bought along water fronts where seamen foregather: a small leather sack, loaded with shot and suspended from a wrist-strap.

At the extreme bottom of the package, carefully preserved between two sheets of thick cardboard, lay a page torn from a newspaper. It was on that heavy, glossed paper which some journals use for their pictorial sections and was covered with miscellaneous illustrations.

I was on the point of throwing the thing away, when some impulse led me to turn it over. What I saw altered and remoulded all my life from that moment forward.

A curtain of dusk was beginning to fall upon the hinterland at the edge of the forest. The fringe of cane and palm was filling up with shadow and the peak of the volcano was brooding against a sky of burnished copper.

When I turned the sheet it was as though I had come face to face with an actual personality where a moment ago there had been nothing animate. Of course it was only because the art of photographer and engraver had ably abetted each other, but the portrait which worthily filled the seven columns of glazed paper was a marvel of lifelike presentment—and of indescribable loveliness.

There are authenticated cases, in plenty, of men who have loved a face seen only in a picture. The Mona Lisa of da Vinci has laid over many beholders the hypnotic spell of the long-dead woman immortalized upon its canvas. Pygmalion loved his Galatea. I fancy that, if the truth were told, I loved in that first flash of view the lady who smiled out at me from the lifelessness of ink and paper. The margins of the sheet had been so close trimmed at the top that no date or caption remained, but beneath, the scissors had left two words: "Miss Frances—" and with these two words I must content myself.

But for the picture itself.

I have already confessed my passionate reverence for beauty. Here before me was beauty of the purest type I have ever been privileged to see. It was not the brush magic of a gifted painter who has caught from a lovely model the charm of line and color and canonized them with idealization. It lacked all the fire with which the palette might have kindled it. It recorded nothing more than the lens had seen, yet its flawlessness required no aid of art and asked no odds of color.

Her clear, young eyes smiled out at me with a miracle of graciousness. Her perfectly curving lips were graver, and if possible sweeter than her eyes. Her chin and throat were exquisitely modeled. Her hair was abundantly massed and heavy. I could guess from the photographic tones that its coils and escaping tendrils of curl, varied in shifting lights between the red warmth of gold and the amber of clear honey.

But what most made this a remarkable photograph was its living quality. So vital was the effect as one looked, that it seemed a palpitant personality of breath and soul. The lips might be trembling on the verge of speech and in the quiet smile hovered a delightful hint of whimsical humor. The whole bearing was queenly with that gracious pride which we characterize as royal when we speak of royalty as something inherently noble. For the accolade of a smile from those lips, in the flesh, a man might undertake all manner of folly. The young woman was in evening dress and at her throat hung a rope of pearls.

Suddenly a transport of rage and a bitterness of contrast possessed me. My hair was matted, my arms and hands raw and blackened with blood and grime. I was the picture of abandoned misery. The satirical gods now set Tantalus-wise before my eyes a picture of beauty and ease and shelter—a pretty woman in the charming fripperies of evening dress.

But while I scowled, her eyes smiled back into my own, challenging in me the vagabond spirit of the whimsical, until I too smiled.

I bowed to the picture.

"You are quite right," I said aloud. "Since it is impossible to alter the situation, the only sane course is to recognize its humor. While we are together here, I shall regard you as a living person. It shall be our effort to turn this poor jest on the high gods who are its authors."

It almost seemed to me that the lips parted and the eyes danced approvingly.

"Frances," I added, "I may call you Frances, may I not, in view of the informality of our circumstances?—you are gorgeous. It was good of you to come to keep me company. I needed you."

The air held a twilight stillness upon which my words fell clamorously. I realized that I had not before spoken aloud for more than a day. Into the ensuing silence came a new and alarming sound. It was half human and incoherent, like a number of voices at a distance. I felt my muscles grow rigid and choked off a half-animal growl that rose involuntarily in my throat. Instinctively I was whipping the revolver from its holster and slipping forward, crouched in the protection of a rock, my eyes turned toward the jungle. Vaguely lurking in the gathering fog of shadow, where the palms began, were some eight or ten figures. It was impossible in the waning light to make out what sort of creatures they were, but they moved with a soft prowling tread that was disquieting. After a little while they melted out of sight, but until past midnight I sat my eyes alertly fixed on the tangled dark, while the low-hung stars paraded across the sky.

---

# CHAPTER IX

## A PORTRAIT AND A TEMPLE

The night, however, passed without event and morning came bathing the empty edge of the forest with crystal freshness. The scene I still had to myself. My morning journey down to the water's edge for food and bathing was made with the most painful caution and I ate without relish.

My world had altered overnight. I was no longer merely shipwrecked but shipwrecked among savages who might adhere to that perverted epicureanism which esteems human fare for its flesh pots. Stories of cannibalism had been plentiful at the captain's table on the *Wastrel*—the value of white heads for decorating native huts had been touched upon. My defense was limited to the six cartridges in the chambers of my revolver and the newly discovered slung-shot.

Meantime I was hideously lonely. I turned the chest on end near the opening of my cavern and spread the newspaper portrait upon it for full inspection. The two upper corners I fastened with the curved and jewelled daggers from Jerusalem.

The days which immediately followed marched slowly and were much alike. It was only in my own state of mind that there was any element of change or development.

The lurking figures did not reappear at the edge of the jungle and I began to hope that they were members of some itinerant band from the opposite side of the island who had chanced upon this locality in their wanderings and might not again return. I was not even positive that they had seen me.

Slowly, weirdly, while I dwelt in uncertainty and suspense the influence of the lady in the picture grew upon me and compelled me. It may have been at first, and doubtless was, a form of auto-hypnosis. Already the seed for such an influence had been planted in the dependence which young Mansfield and myself came to feel for the unknown girl's diary. Now, in utter isolation, I was doubly in need of something to avert my thoughts from channels which go down to madness and despair. The lifelike quality of the portrait made it easier to talk aloud, and as the spell grew I found myself talking with the softness of the lover.

There is a power in the spoken word. The mere act of giving audible expression is a spur to thought. Sitting alone and debating how uncertainly the wretched spark of life sputtered at the wick of my being, I was the craven. When I talked to the picture whose lips smiled as though all the world were brave, I grew ashamed of my terror.

Leaving my cave in the morning to forage and reconnoiter with the pistol at my belt, I would carry with me, as a fragrant memory, the gracious smile of her lips and the royal fearlessness of her eyes. Her image nerved me to endurance; gave me a shoulder touch on normal thought, and enabled me to hold in memory the world for which her evening gown and pearls were symbols—and in deeply morbid moments this saved me from losing my grip. Certainly, it was all an artificial stay—a ludicrous pretense—but it served—and that is the final test of any love or any creed. It served.

As these forces worked, I, at times, forgot that the picture was that of an unknown. Its reality was so strong that it came to stand for some one I had left behind, whom I must live to rejoin; some one inexpressibly dear whose love hung over me and safeguarded me like a powerful talisman. Often, in my broken sleep, I would dream that I was sore beset by a thousand dangers and had fled to my cave as animals have fled to caves since the world began, and that I stood huddling there miserably, awaiting the end. Then, in the dream, she would come out of the picture, as Galatea stepped down from the lifelessness of granite into rosy and animated warmth. My assailants always fell back before her coming and I, despite my terror, would attempt to meet her gallantly. She would open a hidden door in the side of the rock, and lead me through it. And always, in this repeated and unvarying dream, beyond the door we stepped into a brilliantly lighted room where men and women chatted carelessly in evening dress and danced to the tinkle of stringed instruments.

By these degrees the illusion grew until my pretense became a vagary and obsession and to me ceased to be a pretense. I fell back on occultism and told myself that I had succeeded by mere concentration of mind in forcing her to project her astral self across the world, until I had with me her picture and her essence of soul.

Many of life's most sacred and permanent institutions are only fictions, long entertained. My fiction became so real to me that for periods I forgot to question it—then sometimes, at a moment when the illusion was strongest, some impulse of reason would strike in upon and chill me, like a sluicing from a cold bucket. It would come upon me to think of myself as I should have appeared to any unwarned stranger, who had found me talking, even lovemaking, with a sheet of lifeless paper. And from that impersonal view-point I would wonder if my brain had already crumbled to madness and imbecility. The cold sweat would bead my forehead. My finger would creep to the trigger of my pistol and linger there, twitching with the itch of self-destruction. But soon the smiling lips would reassure me; the mood would pass and again I would surrender myself to the pretense which was grateful where the truth was austere and desolate.

I discovered in my tramps about the island's edge that this spot seemed to be the most favored home of the orchid. This monarch of flowers bloomed at the jungle's margin, in an infinite variety of flaunting petals, soft colors and deeply glowing life. No other flower is so ethereal and illusively lovely. None could be more fitted for a tribute to as impalpable a love as I acknowledged. It became a part of my daily program to bring back with me as I returned to the cave, masses of these splendid blossoms which I heaped before her shrine.

I had reached the age of thirty-five and had heretofore been immune to feminine fascinations. I had even been characterized as a woman-hater, though this was an injustice. This new obsession, bewitching—whatever you may choose to term it—was not momentary. In defense of my consistency I declare that the thing required two weeks at least for its accomplishment. And in those two weeks other affairs were developing.

Of course, I had been told, as has every traveler in the south seas, that there is not an atoll or island left for discovery. I had been informed that on every coral speck in the reef-strewn ocean, there is or has been, a white man. I knew now that this was a fallacy. My island was marked by a volcano tall enough to proclaim itself as far as a glass could sweep the horizon from a ship's lookout, and if no pearl shell or beche-de-mer trader, no blackbirder of the old days, no windswept vessel of the present had hitherto sighted that peak, it must lie too far off the course of rambling traffic, to expect a visit now. I knew that we had dropped down-world for days before the wreck, and I had heard grumbling, because of the mysterious course being steered. I was the firstcomer—and yet the faint and struggling instinct of hope urged the setting up of a tattered flag or two of sail cloth along the beetling heights.

From my eyrie in the rocks, the coast line went away in a succession of broken and porous cliffs which I had explored for a distance of perhaps two miles. That two miles held all I had learned to know of this island which was clearly a large one. What the interior had behind its curtain of palm and moss and cane—back in the impenetrable jungle—belonged to the mystery of an unopened book. I did know that off to the left as one faced the sea, separated from me by four or five miles of precipitous coast line, loomed a headland from which a flag waving by day would be observable—if ever a vessel came across the shoulder of the world. To reach the point and return would be a day's journey, for the path I must take led over a trail more suited to a mountain goat than a man who had until lately been civilized.

One morning I set out carrying tightly wrapped one of the pieces of sail-cloth which had come out of the mate's chest. My resolution to set my flag flying had filled me with a sort of specious exaltation. The venomous beauty of the place was beyond description, and in a measure I yielded to its lure and walked almost buoyantly. The sea to its skyline was blue with a depth of sapphire. The tangle of the jungle was aflash with vivid and sparkling color. Small, harmless snakes slid brightly aside, as multi-hued as shreds of rainbow. I had climbed and crawled for several hours, and was beginning to suffer keenly from weariness and stone bruises on my poorly protected feet, when I came to a sort of path running upward. This led me to a more commanding eminence than I had before reached and gave me a view inland over an endless blanket of green, unbroken forest. Ahead of me was a still greater height, and after a short rest I made my way to the point from which I could look across its crest. Then I halted dead in my tracks and stood fingering my revolver. A cold sweat came out on my forehead and my knees trembled, threatening to fail me. It was as though a curtain had risen on a stage set to terrify the beholder.

The high ground fell steeply away into a basin whose slopes were roughly broken into rising tiers. These tiers commanded a sort of amphitheatre two hundred yards in diameter, through which ran a small thread of water cascading from the interior elevation. A quarter of a mile away began the background of timber and tangle.

The bottom of the basin had been worn smooth by much treading. A boulder some four feet tall and probably of an equal thickness rose, pulpit like, at the center. Its top was hollowed out into a bowl and its sides were inscribed with crude hieroglyphics. Near it were a half-dozen upright poles, surmounted by what seemed to be cocoanuts. In a dozen places under rude stone ovens were the ashes of dead fires. Scattering piles of human bones—but nowhere a skull—told me that I had stumbled on a *kai-kai* temple—a place of cannibal observances and feasting. I did not at once venture into the hollow for closer scrutiny. It was not such an institution as one would care to invade carelessly. Over the whole place hung a horrible stench. Flies buzzed about it in noisy, filthy swarms. After a long interval of listening and reconnoitering I became convinced that this place of special observance was to-day as neglected as are many churches in Christian lands on week days.

I crept tremblingly down into the abominable pit and made my way toward the stone altar prepared now for any atrocious sight. But the climax of discovery came when I had crawled half way and the cocoanuts on the poles resolved themselves into withered, human heads, sun dried and yellow fringed.

These mummied skulls were for the most part trophies of old battles, but lying at the top of the rock was another which must have surmounted its living shoulders only a few days ago. The frizzled hair was tied into dozens of kinky knots. The facial angle was low and slanting and the coarse lips were hideously twisted in a snarl of death and defiance. On the scalp, which a war club had crushed, sat a very beautiful head-dress of gull feathers, brilliantly dyed in green and crimson and orange. The victim had worn to his obsequies such a decoration as might have crowned a princess of the Incas. He had been a warrior of rank and now, as befitted his station, his head lay drying out on a mat of yellow and brown wood pulp.

A stifling nausea assaulted the pit of my stomach. My retreating steps reeled drunkenly, and when, near the rim of the basin, I turned for a final gaze in the fascination of horror, I no longer had the place to myself.

Two human figures stood at the farther rim of the amphitheater, silently regarding me. Both were thin, pigmy-built men with long arms and low foreheads. Their faces, grotesquely disfigured with bone and shell ornaments spiked through noses and ears, were bestial yet not stupid. Their eyes were beady and sharp, and just now their thick lips hung pendulous with wonderment. For an instant I was incapable of motion; then, as they stood in equal petrification, I remembered and acted on the counsel of an east-side gang member whom I had once been privileged to know in New York. I had inconsequently inquired whether, in his acrimonious career, he never came eye to eye with fear.

"Sure thing," he had promptly replied, "but when a guy gets your goat—stall. If you makes de play strong enough it's a cinch you gets his goat too."

By that rule this was my moment to "stall." I drew myself up to the limit of stature and threw out my chest in the best semblance of arrogance I could assume.

They were decked like the head of their sacrificial victim, in brilliant feather work, beautifully and harmoniously wrought. Their flint-tipped spears were elaborately carved and their necklaces were fashioned of shells and teeth. Some of the teeth were human. For perhaps thirty seconds we held the strained tableau, then I glanced over my shoulder. Between me and retreat stood a third figure. Compared to his gaudiness of decking, the raiment of the others was mean and sober. One bare shoulder and arm was covered with festering ulcers. His monkey-like face had the same slant of brow and heaviness of lip, but it worked constantly with a keen and twitching play of expression which argued speculative thought. As I turned he was leaning on a knotted war-club, and regarding me with profound gravity.

# CHAPTER X

## I SEEK ORCHIDS

Internally I was quaking, and thinking very fast. The first shock of their astonishment was dissipating, and two of the three faces were clouding into a glowering scrutiny which augured darkly for my escape. The gaze of the third held a grave perplexity, touched with awe, and in the interval of overcharged silence the other eyes dwelt questioningly on his.

I knew from their spell-bound attitudes that I was the first white man they had seen and an apparition. Measured by their pigmy standards, I was a gigantic being of a new type and order, possibly I was even immortal.

As a man they had no fear of me. The revolver which I had slipped from its holster and cocked had not impressed them. They knew nothing of its death-dealing quality. That was a point in my favor. It would afford, if need be, six miracles of mortality, but the jungle that had disgorged them could disgorge hundreds of others like them—perhaps thousands. Gods must carry themselves, when they walk among men, with a godlike scorn of mundane dangers. I turned to the one man who was above the others, exposing my back to the two spears, as though safe in my consciousness of immunity. I extended one arm with a gesture intended to epitomize great majesty. It was a pose borrowed from some old sculptor's conception of the Olympian Zeus—albeit shamefully exaggerated.

It was an anxious moment. Should he, to whom I made my commanding plea, lift his finger in signal, the spears from behind, poisoned spears perhaps, would strike me down. But as I strode forward, with one hand still pointing heavenward, I commanded him in a mighty voice to stand aside.

He on his part eyed me dubiously, never shifting his attitude or raising his club from the earth, but he permitted me to pass from the amphitheatre unmolested. I went, deliberately, holding my gaze rigidly to the front and using every ounce of self-control to curb the impulse of my feet to run, and the impulse of my neck to crane. A vestige of misgiving, a note of human anxiety, would have destroyed me.

My peril was superlative, and yet as I look back on the occasion, I can see that it overdid comedy and became pure farce. I was defending my life with burlesque. My audience would not be impressed by finesse, and impressing it was a matter of life and death. In the words of the east-side bruiser, I was "makin' it strong."

At all events my bearing, in a situation without precedent of etiquette, found sufficient favor to cover my retreat and I went down to the sea unfollowed. I had none the less seen enough to set me thinking and thought brought little solace. Were I accepted on the basis of my own divine assumption, and regarded as a being from another world, the story would travel fast among their villages. Its wonder would be promulgated and men would burn with curiosity to behold me. Among those who came as pilgrims would be some demanding proofs and miracles. I was now committed to a permanent policy of bluff. I had always been regarded as a facetious individual. Now my life depended on attaining a supreme flippancy of attitude on pain of sacrifice to rites for which I had no reverence. When at sundown I reached the place where the portrait smiled whimsically at me from its post of honor, I sat for a while looking into the comprehending eyes and my thoughts took more cheerful color. Before me lay a situation in which I was to pit my legacy of human development against the brute odds of minds lighted only to the mistiness of dawn.

"Frances," I said, "you smile. Of course since you are fixed in print, you can't do otherwise than smile. I wonder—" I broke off and became suddenly and unaccountably serious. "I wonder if you would smile, were you here with me in the flesh as well as merely in the spirit. I wonder if you would."

Then with a feeling which was tremendously real, I added fervently and aloud, "Thank God you are not here in the flesh—but I am grateful for your smiling. Somehow I find it reassuring."

After a little reflection I summarized the entire situation to the lady with whom I discussed my affairs.

"You see, my dear," I informed her, "to their untutored and man-eating minds I present a dilemma. I am either a great immortal, whom it would be most unwise to heckle—or I am very good eating, in which case it is a pity to let me grow thinner."

"It shall be our care, dear lady," I added, "to maintain this status of godship and to that end we must arrange a little program of simple miracles from time to time. You see," I explained, "it won't be long before they will be coming here and demanding what manner of deity I am, and what is my immortal name. Do you know what I shall tell them?"

I paused and grinned into the smiling eyes and the lips that seemed trembling on the verge of speech.

"I shall tell them," I assured her, "that in me they behold the great god Four-flush."

If I concede to the cold logic of material reasoning that this dependable companionship and love of a man for a portrait washed up by the sea was merely the aberration of a brain unseated by solitude, I must also believe that a series of totally incredible coincidences subsequently befell me. But if it be that certain things are written in the stars and certain passions are irrevocably decreed, my life is freed of grotesqueness and becomes logical.

While I lived under the sword of the problematical to-morrow, suspended by the hair of an uncertain to-day, my dependence upon her grew greater. The brave man is said to die once and the coward often, but the line between the courage and cowardice is not absolute. There were periods when I felt that I could play the game and die if I must, with the detached philosophy of a Socrates. At other times I wallowed in the pit of foreboding and died several times a day. In these moods I wished for the moment of crisis which should put my resolution to the touch, and end the matter.

The savages did not approach my cave, but sometimes when evening fell and the jungle spread itself in a fringed blanket against the moonlight, I could make out skulking patches of shadow at its edge. In my rambles too I had a sense of being endlessly watched by unseen eyes, and once bending over a sunlit pool to drink, I was startled by the haggard face which looked up from it with streaks of white in its long, tangled hair. Each day I brought fresh orchids from the jungle's edge and heaped them before my intangible lady.

"They are more beautiful, Frances," I told her, "than any I could buy you along the Champs Elysées or Fifth Avenue—and all they cost is a ship and crew and cargo."

One morning I discovered that where the growth of cane and moss and vines had formerly been thick and unbroken there were now several clearly defined alleyways, made by the coming and going of the blacks, bent on observing me. A few inquisitive steps into one of these trails revealed, at a little distance, a pool of water. Its basin was of mossy rock, and its edges were choked with ferns. A slender waterfall fed it, and through the cloistered half-light of the forest interior fell a few fervid dashes of sunlight like gold leaf on the somber tones of greenery. The air hung wet and steamy like the atmosphere of a hot house. But the marvel of it was the orchids. They climbed and trailed and illumined the place with a dozen varieties of weird and subtle beauty. One could understand why men take their lives into their hands and penetrate fever-infested jungles in search of newer types. Their delicacy was unearthly and splendid. They were not, it seemed, flowers growing on dirt-fed stems, but blossoms of the gods. Each one was like the blooming of some human soul freed from the grossness of the flesh. Here was a bloom as ethereally pure and pale as the reincarnation of some flawless virgin spirit; there were flaming petals of such magnificent color as might have sprung from the heart of a conqueror. I saw epitomized in petal and stamen, all the poetry of the world's dead dreams. I took as many as I could carry back to the portrait, and on the following morning I returned for more.

They lured me strangely with their fox fire of sheer beauty, until I had penetrated the jungle to the distance of a quarter of a mile and stood in a small opening where I plucked an armful of their blossoms.

Suddenly, as I started back, I felt a biting pang in my left shoulder, and knew that I had been speared, though the tangle of the jungle revealed no human form, and its silence remained unbroken. The spear, which had come from nowhere, as it seemed, fell to the ground, but not before it had gashed my flesh and left upon the tattered remnants of my jacket a tell-tale smear of blood.

I believed myself to have been mortally poisoned by the javelin, and my one wish now was to escape, with the semblance of greatness still upon me, and die unseen. I went with as much dignity as possible toward the beach, backing through the tangle to keep my flow of blood concealed. I had no doubt that many unseen eyes followed my exit and even if it were for a brief time, I wished to go with the seeming of divine invulnerability. I even forced a loud and derisive shout of laughter which rang weirdly through the silences. Wicked pains shot in white-hot currents through my blood and racked my muscles. I was weak with nauseating pain and dizziness swam in my brain. At last the merciful rocks gave me concealment. I dropped on my knees, my teeth gritted, and dragged myself back to my cave where I turned my face to the rock wall to die.

---

# CHAPTER XI

## I FIND MYSELF A DEMI-GOD

Yet I did not die. While I lay waiting to do so the insistent ache of my bones, the racking of my wound and the sodden numbness of my brain, slowly blurred me into apathy. That passed and the delirium came on a swelling tide of temperature. Centuries trampled roughshod over me and demons of pain scourged me through the seven hells of fever. Scorching wastes of time were broken at long intervals by little oases of lucidity when I crawled to the opening and drank, but even these were clouded by shreds of nightmare horror, and remembered hallucinations.

Once, waking to momentary sensibility, I found the narrow cave still ringing with the echoes of my tortured and delirious shrieks.

When, at last, I came fully to myself, painfully weak and scalded with the fever, but sane, I could see the stars spangling my scrap of sky. My adventure had occurred in the morning, but whether hours or days had played out their scores I did not know. I drank and slept again. I next woke to the glare of forenoon. The clouds in my brain had been swept away, and the hand I lifted fell weakly back on a forehead which was cool and moist. The battling life spark had triumphed over the native poison. But when I tried to drag myself to the mouth of my grotto, my weak head began rambling again, so that real and unreal things wandered strangely together. My side was lacerated by the pistol which had been at my belt as I tossed in the fever. A twist in the fissure brought me to the point where I, still concealed in the dark shadow, could see the primitive terrace of my plateau, and there were such things as brought back upon me an avalanche of terror, rage and violence.

The lady still smiled from her post of honor with her gracious and fearless eyes. The curved damascus daggers still held the enamelled sheet in place, but beyond her I saw death. Against a background of intense sea and sky under the glare of a fiercely brilliant sun, stood grouped a human ensemble of indescribable color and savagery. Upon scores of black and sweating torsos; upon gorgeously dyed feather work and shell ornaments, the light fell in color gone mad. They stood massed and silent, their spears and bows and clubs for the moment idle. Their faces mutilated with spiked ears and nose ornaments and dyed teeth, were unspeakably hideous. Every eye was just now intent on the portrait of my lady. At the front stood the three whom I had supposed to be priests at the amphitheatre, and with them was a man very aged and white haired, but erect and gorgeously appareled.

Slowly one of the priests approached the portrait and put out an ulcerous hand to touch the face. A tidal wave of unspeakable fury caught me up and swept me back into the realm of insanity. I was transplanted in an instant to the nightmares of my delirium. I saw instead of a lifeless picture the slender, breathing figure of the woman I worshiped contaminated by this profane touch. I attempted to rush out and die like some Mad Mullah devotee in fanatical battle with her assailants, but my strength was not equal to my impulse. I stumbled to my knees and my right hand fell upon the hilt of my pistol. I whipped it out and fired. In my agued hand it should have been harmless enough, but the range was short and I had once been a marksman. I saw the man crumple forward with a short, strangled groan. I saw those at the back crowding one another over the cliff in the panic of their disordered flight. They had not seen me. They knew only that bolts of death were striking them down. I heard endless thunders as the pistol report sent its echoes beating and rebounding against the confined walls of the fissure. Blue and slender lines of spiraling smoke went drifting out into the air. I caught a glimpse of two bolder spirits stopping to drag away their dead. Then I collapsed and lay for hours where I had fallen.

Once more I awoke with a moist forehead and a hunger which gnawed at the pit of my stomach. Only the gods knew how long I had been without food. The air fanned me with the soft, reviving breath of night. The moon, riding up the east made an irregular diagram of silvered light across the ledge, and fell with a reassuring touch of ivoried white, on the newspaper sheet and the portrait.

I was too famished and spent to stand, but I made the journey down to the beach on hands and knees, and when I had eaten my fill of unsavory crabs I lay for a time in the grateful coolness of the wet sand and drew new strength from its healing. My sickness was ended. The pitiable weakness that had made the downward journey a torture was the heritage of hunger. I had needed no medicine but food, and now I found myself able to walk back upright. That night I slept sweetly and dreamed once again of the familiar door beyond which lay luxury and security.

The sun was high when I awoke with a sense of great refreshment and recovery. The slit of sky framed in the rift was not yet hot, but tenderly blue with a color of promise. The fronds of fern and palm stirred to the land breeze. I went down to my surf bath and breakfast with an almost buoyant step. A half-hour after my return, when I turned to look at the jungle edge a sight greeted me which demonstrated the decision of the natives that our intercourse was not so soon to become a closed incident.

This time, however, their coming was characterized by a more gratifying element of respect. They swarmed out of the bush, not in paltry dozens nor scores, but in their panoplied hundreds. Gorgeously decked chiefs and the club-bearing warriors smeared with indigo halted in the open, leaving a satisfying interval between their position and mine. With great and conspicuous show of peace the warriors discarded their spears and shields and raised their weaponless hands for me to behold as I looked down from my high place. The white-haired king broke a spear, gazing up at me the while, then dropping the pieces knelt and bowed his slanting forehead to the sands. At his back bent the priests, trailing their bright feathers in the dust. No one could misunderstand their pantomime. Men of their tribe had offended the deities. A nation had come in humility and supplication for forgiveness.

While they made obeisance in relays a group of young men approached the priests, bearing armfuls of orchids. The king and priests and orchid-bearers moved forward for a few steps and halted, gazing up inquiringly at me. This performance was several times repeated before I understood that they were seeking my consent to approach nearer. Then I bowed and pointed inward. A rigorous order of precedence was observed, the aged king keeping his place at their head and his followers their positions of relative rank. The weight of his years made the royal steps so slow that the colorful pageant crept like an army of snails.

Suddenly it dawned upon me that if I were to be a god receiving a delegation of mortals, I should receive it in some suitable degree of state. They were sending to me the mightiest men of their villages. The kinky head of their king was abased. Aged Merlins were coming on their marrow bones, resplendently trailing their feathered finery along the white and flaring sands. I stood awaiting them in a raveled, mud-smeared suit of pajamas which at their best had never been ostentatious. The thing seemed unfit. Evidently these folk inclined to the splendor of pomp. Jeffersonian simplicity would be lost on them. Their pageant should be met with pageantry. There had been some who had doubted and denied me. Of a surety if I were to play this nabob from the skies; if I were to turn the averted tragedy into a screaming and cheerful farce, it was my duty to dress the part.

With a signal of raised hands, I signified that they were to await my reappearance. Then I bowed with profound dignity, and stepping from their view, disappeared.

A few minutes later I emerged from my cave, a transmogrified being. I was no longer the derelict of rags and tatters. Mine was the opulent splendor of a High Mandarin of China. About my fever-wasted frame fell and flapped the gorgeous folds of the embroidered kimono. In my hands I carried a violin and bow. It is true I was unshaven, and through holes in my canvas shoes protruded eight or ten toes, but what mortal can assume to criticise such eccentricities as may be the part of godhood?

When I took my stand once more on my pedestal of mountain, I found them patiently awaiting the nod of deity. The sun fell resplendently on my silver storks and gold dragons and silk poppies. The lessening land breeze fluttered the embroidery-crusted folds and splintered light from my person. I listened with satisfaction to the incoherent sound that went up from many throats; a chorused gasp of profound awe and admiration and wonderment.

I signaled my immortal readiness to receive them. As the ludicrousness of the farce broke over me I had to bite back unsolemn roars of laughter. A spirit of deviltry and vaudeville possessed me. As their high priests in deadly earnest marched on all fours with faces as rapt and fanatically sober as those of Mecca pilgrims, I drew the bow across the catgut and, lifting my voice, proclaimed myself in ragtime.

I informed them in the words which were new only to them and solemn only to them that I had rings on my fingers and bells on my toes, and as I sung they became hushed with awe and approached with a deeply moved sense of their great honor and responsibility.

When they were only a little way off, I went down to meet them, and with a condescension which I trusted would not injure my prestige, lifted the aged chieftain to his feet and permitted him to walk. He, however, remained deferentially two paces in my rear. It was evident from their straining upward gazes, that deeply as they were moved to reverence by my own exalted spectacle, there was some greater revelation which they awaited above. This disquieted me since I had in reserve no added climax to offer. I had given them a display savoring of the circus but I had no grand spectacle to advertise in the main tent after the regular performance.

When we had reached the plateau, however, I understood and was relieved. To me they had come kneeling, but before Her portrait they threw themselves on their faces and groveled. They sprinkled sand and pebbles upon their hair and their voices, even to me who understood no syllable, carried such depth of humility and supplication as filled me with wonder.

They would rise from their suppliance only long enough to glance at the face of the picture, then fall again and renew their paroxysms of ungainly prayer. From the hands of the orchid-bearers they took the heaps of blooms, and piled them at a distance from the shrine. The young men who had been so signally honored withdrew from the holy of holies. Only the high priests and the king were left with me in the sacred arena.

For a time I stood dumbly looking on, then the idea percolated into my confused understanding. I realized that at best I was only a demi-god, perhaps a sort of super-high-priest, but no god. These ambassadors extraordinary had come not to me but to The Lady of the Portrait.

I lifted up my voice for attention, and from their kneeling postures they regarded me with grave reverence. I took my place, with bowed head, before the portrait and addressed the lady in tones of deep solemnity. It seemed to me that her delicate mouth line quivered with amusement, as though she and I had between us a delicious secret.

"Frances! Frances! Frances!" I declaimed with the deep profundity of a ritual. "I have failed totally and signally at the god job. There is in all this world of sky and sea and of my heart but one deity. It was you who struck down with a thunderbolt the sacrilegious, false priest. It was you who saved me from death and raised me to the high estate of your vicegerent." I paused and went on more seriously: "It is you whom these people worship with idolatry—and of them all, none worships you so wholly as I, your priest!" And though I was declaiming before a lifeless image to impress ignorant cannibals, I meant it. When I had finished there rose a devout murmur from the blacks, and with a motion to them to remain, I went into the cave and came out again with the small Japanese burner and a taper of incense. As the heavy fragrance of the burning stuff spread itself upon the air, their wonder grew.

---

**"Frances! Frances! Frances!" I declaimed with the deep profundity of a ritual.**

---

At length I wheeled and pointed back to the jungle. Slowly, reluctantly, but with perfect obedience, the wild bush men took up their backward journey to relate the unbelievable tale of their reception.

---

# CHAPTER XII

## PORT AND STARBOARD LIGHTS

There are men whose lives develop in gradations of gentle growth. Decade merges into decade by unstartling evolution. Variations of thread and color run smoothly into the life-pattern. With me it has been otherwise. The constantly recurring dream of the portal in the cliff was in a fashion symbolical of my life. The dreamed-of rescue never came by degrees, but by the abrupt opening of a door where there had been no door before and by the sudden changing of worlds in a step across the threshold. For me epoch had followed epoch with sudden breaks and few connecting threads. One day I was a bored tourist lounging under the striped awnings of Shepheard's Hotel. The next day found me on a disreputable ocean tramp bound for the Ultima Thule. That voyage had ended as suddenly as it began—with a quick curtain of unconsciousness on a tableau of violence. Mansfield, too, dropped out of my life with more instant suddenness that he had entered it. Now, presto! with the sudden trickeries of a mountebank the sprite who played with my destinies ushered in another unprefaced era. Across an invisible line I stepped into days of luxury and prosperity.

It is told that the Inca god-kings breakfasted each morning on fruit fresh plucked from growing-places a hundred miles away. In a horseless land relays of runners, each dashing his appointed distance, saw to it that a perishable dainty outlived its journey across a mountain range. This gives a key to my mode of existence, for several months following, though my luxury was of a lesser scale. In those months I mastered some vocabulary— and in so crude a dialect vocabulary suffices. I lacked fluency, of course, and had trouble with their consonant-locked syllables and gutturals, but in a fashion I could talk. Day followed day with a monotony of ease. I was no longer satisfied with the noisome flesh of disgusting crabs, and gull eggs far advanced toward the hatching. Delicacies of fish and flesh and hitherto unheard-of fruits were served up to me to satiation. My tattered pajamas gave way to garments of cocoa-fiber and feathered finery for ceremonial wear. The necessity of entering into the lives of the natives brought repulsive revelations which I endured as best I could since if I were to influence them I must proceed with a nice diplomacy. My "fluttered folk and wild" could not be hurriedly herded into new folds. Departing spirits, they believed, followed the sun into the west. Gods visited mortals though usually in invisible forms and were fond of the flesh of enemies slain in battle. Fetich and superstition took a hundred phases. Their gusty and savage minds were childishly susceptible and in their quickly roused affections they were as demonstrative as collies. I began shortly to look about for some simple miracle wherein the new goddess might manifest herself as a deity of benefaction as well as of condign punishment. The opportunity came in a fashion most unexpected and the result hardly made for a reform of enlightenment. I was told that there dwelt in stilt-supported villages of grass on the far side of the island a warlike tribe, with whom my people were hostile.

My folk were bushmen and dreaded the sea, but these enemies were salt-water men, who could with axe and adz scoop from the solid tree outrigger canoes and who were terrible in their strength. Their king was lord over several villages and about his house went (this they told me with bated breath) a row of many round stones, and each stone stood for an enemy slain and eaten. For many seasons there had been peace, but one day there arrived at my plateau a delegation of grief-torn warriors. A small village had been attacked and two heads taken to swell the row of stones around the canoe house. They had now come to propitiate the deity bearing fruits and exquisitely wrought spears. They besought the forgiveness of my Gracious Lady, because they could offer no enemies' flesh—the most god-satisfying of sacrifices. This omission, however, they swore to remedy, if victory were permitted to hover over them in fight. Among the most devout of the petitioners was Ra Tuiki, the aged chief with white hair. They urged me to accompany them to their principal village and lay the hand of blessing on their clubs and spears.

Through dense tangles of palm and fern, mangrove and moss I was borne in a rough hammock of fiber. Great soft-winged butterflies flapped across the course of our march. Brilliant birds fluttered off, twittering and screaming. I should have preferred walking, but my position prohibited it. To condescend meant to become a mere man.

In their squalid villages of grass hovels I found filth and the excitement of battle preparation. It was my first view of their home life—and my last. I was taken to the house of a chief or sub-king, who lay mortally hurt of an arrow wound, and who wished to have the blessing of the highest priest that his spirit might take its course honorably, and without curse, to the west. He lay on his mat dying, and was older and more repulsive to the eye than Ra Tuiki. His ears had been stretched by many huge ornaments, and the cartilage of his nose was torn and ragged where the chances of battle had pulled out rings and spikes. His eager eyes gazed up at me out of a face stiffened and set with elephantiasis, and by his mat lay, unwrapped from their fiber coverings, that they might comfort his passing spirit, two excellently preserved negroid heads. I shuddered, but I laid my hand on his slanting forehead—and I have seen men die with less dignity.

As night brought the closing in of choking jungle shadows, a half-dozen red fires leaped up to drive their ribbons of red flare into the blackness. They wavered fitfully and grotesquely upon twisting, leaping bodies, which were paradoxically preparing for the ordeal of the morrow by hideous orgies and dances and fatigue and nerve waste. But when the first light of sunrise attacked the reek of dew that veiled the jungle, while the dying fires still smouldered into gray ash and my throat labored in stifling gasps of wet, they trailed out silently into the bush. They were a long line of shadow shapes whose footfall made no sound, and whose pigmy bodies melted into the tangle as impalpably as the dissipating mists. My bearers carried me back to the shore. Two days later their delegation came chattering in hysterical delight and bringing in native triumph the head of the king who had three hundred stones about his house.

About this time I instituted an important policy. By night I had signal fires kept burning on every high place along the coast. I disingenuously told my people that where a great shrine is, there must also be at nightfall mighty banners of flame. They liked the idea. Despite their hideous ferocity, they liked everything which might have appealed to the imagination of a child. They liked music, they liked color. The greatest privilege that their warriors could earn, was that of coming, to the number of a dozen at a time, to my plateau by night and after due reverence of squatting for hours on their haunches, while I coaxed from the violin airs from opera or music hall.

On the point above us blazed one of our signal fires, and between the reddened crevices of rock its flare struck down and yellowed our gathering. The portrait would catch the light and leap from its shadow. Over us were the stars. In a circle of silent absorption sat dark immovable figures, with high lights gleaming, here and there, on the mahogany of cheek-bone or forehead. Some fantastic painter might portray these gatherings on canvas. He would need a bold brush. I find no words for its description, but fantastic it was and strange. Under the fetich of the starlight I would find myself drifting away into realms of storied romance with the woman I loved and had not seen. Then my bow would all unconsciously drift into love songs. I would find myself singing—"Ever the wide world over, lass"—and oftentimes when my voice rose to the strain I could fancy that She joined me in its singing. Her voice sang in my brain definitely and with the sweetness of the beloved and familiar. I had, of course, never heard a syllable from her lips, and yet I was sure that could I hear her voice in life I should instantly recognize it, though blindfolded. I thought of it as a richly sweet contralto. It never for a moment occurred to me to fancy it might be anything else.

Once for a week the sky ceased to smile, and grew black. The jungle was lashed and stripped with hurricanes and on several occasions the earth trembled. The sea pounded our porous coast and boiled into a tremendous tide. I knew that if the cyclonic scope was general, ships were having trouble, but in that thought lurked a vague hope. If any power were to drive a vessel to my rescue it would be a power which carried sailors out of their ordered courses. One night, some six months after the wreck of the *Wastrel*, when the skies were serene again I found myself more than ordinarily adrift on the tide of imagination. The march of the stars showed that midnight had passed, and yet the natives sat unhurried, and I, as unhurried as they, was still absorbed with the violin.

My eyes traveled out to sea, absently and without reason. Suddenly the bow stopped half-way across the strings with a rasping gasp of the catgut. The instrument itself fell from my hands and I sat rigid and staring like a man suddenly stricken. The other eyes followed mine and also remained riveted. Leagues away over the phosphorescent waste of water, but clear and unblinking, glowed the green spot of a ship's starboard light. I tried to speak, but for the moment my grasp on their dialect slipped from me and left me dumb. I was trembling with heart-bursting excitement, and at sight of my emotion they began to stir uneasily with a threat of panic.

As suddenly as it had left me my self-possession returned. With a sweeping gesture I pointed to the myriad stars that gemmed the heavens and told them that one of these had come down to the sea, bringing other demi-gods like myself. I adjured them to build up the fires of welcome until the island might seem a mountain of flame. Their strongest men must feed, as never fires had before been fed, and all others must go to their huts and await the morrow.

Alone on my plateau I saw the fires leap up in a coast-wise line of beacons that dyed the night vermilion. The tiny point of seaward green was crawling snail-like on the sea and at last my gaze was rewarded by a slender flowering spray of rocket fire, followed by another and another. Then the point of light ceased crawling and stood still. I let my head fall forward in my palms and my breath came in spasmodic gasps.

But as I raised my eyes they fell on the smiling lips of the portrait. It seemed to me that Her lips and eyes, still gracious, even congratulatory, held a touch of wistful sadness which had not been there before. They seemed such lips and eyes as say, "*Bon voyage* and farewell."

The glow of wine-like exultation died in my arteries and a chill settled on my heart. There, in the world of tangible things and unrelenting facts, what room would there be for such a companionship? Was this strongest love of my life to melt into nothing now that I no longer needed its support? Was it a dream? If so it was a dream from which I should awake to an empty life. No! I would set out to find her in the flesh. I halted my reflections with a start. And when I found her—what? I sat there in the midst of silences, and the sweep of essential things. About me lay leagues of sea, miles of rock, an infinity of sky. They brooded gigantically over me and whispered that there are mysterious influences greater than man's cold facts. Man's thought became only a fluttering stir in a center of protoplasm. I was as near to the beginnings of things as to the present. It was as easy to believe in the love of souls that had not met as in other matters.

"No—no!" I cried out, bending before the face, "Whatever it be, there are loves great enough to burn into miracles. This is not the first time I have loved you—nor the last. Through æons of reincarnation a love like this runs on." I paused awhile, then added, with an effort to smile. "Don't you remember even one or two former lives, dear?

"'... happy we lived and happy we lovedAnd happy at last we died;And deep in the rift of a Caradoc driftWe slumbered side by side.The world turned on in the lathe of time,The hot sands heaved amain,Till we caught our breath from the womb of deathAnd crept into light again.'"

My eyes were fixed so tensely on the portrait that it grew blurred. Slowly it seemed to me to vanish and in its place stood a real and living figure. I could give no detail of its dress or coloring, but it was a figure of marvelous beauty, and it gazed into my eyes and shook its head. Then it faded and I was looking again at the portrait. There was a choke in my throat, and, falling to my knees, I kissed the printed lips.

---

# CHAPTER XIII

## ENTER THE INFANTRYMAN

The morning would bring by rescuers and the breaking up of housekeeping in my cave. I had no wish that profane eyes should look upon the portrait or the devout worship of my beloved cannibals. Now that I was leaving them I realized that they were beloved. In my memory loomed a hundred acts of simple courtesy. The portrait I took down from its shrined position; the Damascus daggers I put again into their places, and the Mandarin's kimono I folded carefully into a package. On all these things, as on the era for which they stood, I dropped the lid of the mate's chest.

The morning came on brilliant and fresh with the cleansing sweep of the trades. Sky and sea sparkled in a diamond clarity, and below me on the beach patiently waited the dignitaries of my tribe in festal regalia. Since this was our parting, I too came out decked in the finery of bird plumage. I did not allow them to climb to the now empty shrine, but led them down with me to the beach, where shortly a boat came bobbing over the water.

A queer enough spectacle we must have made, like a flock of blackbirds patched with the oriole's vermilion and the cockatoo's rose. I myself, burned out of my Caucasian birthright, differed from them only in my size.

For a time the handful of white men on the boat hesitated to risk the chances of landing and being *kai-kai'd*. As they circled at a distance I made my throat raw, shouting reassurances in English, while my wondering blacks contemplated with deep awe this talking of the gods.

At last the rescuers rowed in, and I waded out waist deep to meet them. The officer in command was a colossal Scotchman with a ruddy face and an honest mouth as stiffly sober as though it had never yielded to the seduction of a smile. He gave me a detail of two kanakas whose brawny arms carried down the chest and its contents.

At last came the moment I had dreaded. I must break the news to these waiting children that the priests from the stars had not come to bring them new and permanent wonders, but to take back to the lands of mystery their goddess and myself. I wished then for a full knowledge of their tongue, that I might soften the tidings, but I could not bring myself to the mendacity of promising a return, though they pleaded. When it came to parting with Ra Tuiki, I forgot my quasi-divinity and seized the old head-hunter's hand in an ungodlike, Anglo-Saxon grip.

Their island would now be charted. Missionaries would come to them with teachings of a new faith, but treading on their heels would come men of another sort, and as I thought of these I wished that we might be able to leave the place unchronicled. The contract trader would soon arrive, supported if need be by the authority of his flag's navy, bringing to my cannibals, or some of them, long terms of peonage under hard plantation masters.

"What, if I may ask," suggested the solemn-visaged Scot at the helm, when the bow was turned outward and the boat crew was bending to the oars, "was all the demonstration of th' niggers?"

"They were saying good-bye," I explained, "We came to have a very satisfactory understanding."

He pondered my answer for a time in sober silence, then dismissed the matter with a single observation.

"They took it cruel hard, sir."

Over the side of the *Gretchen* I went to a kindly reception. I told all of my story that I wished to tell, admitting that I had posed as a sort of demi-god, but breathing no hint of the godship which was over my priesthood.

A week of hurricane and storm had tested the ship's endurance, exhausted the crew, and driven the *Gretchen* into unknown waters.

"If it hadn't been for your signal fires," the captain told me, "we might have gone to smash on the outlying needles. Your lights probably saved us as well as yourself."

This was no larger ship than the *Wastrel*, but when one went to his berth at night it was with confidence that his sleep would not be interrupted by the sudden necessity of getting up to die. She had carried a cargo of trade stuffs south and was returning to Singapore by way of Brisbane, laden with copra and pearl shell. Her direction lay westerly while I wished to go east, but that was secondary. At the Australian port, I could reship. Indeed, I was told our course might shortly cross that of a regular line of steamers between Brisbane and Honolulu. For a few days it was satisfying enough to pick up the lost ends of the world's stale news. While I had been marking time the world had been marching; a hundred paragraphs had been lived into history.

On the fourth day a slender thread of smoke rose over the western horizon which grew into a clean-painted and white-cabined steamer. As the gap closed white-clad men and even women stood crisply out against the deck-rail. Then with much signaling from the halyards the two vessels had converse of which I was the subject, and I with my chest went over the side of the *Gretchen*. I told the steamer's purser as much of my story as I had told on the *Gretchen*, and when that evening I appeared at the captain's table transformed by bathing in a real tub and submission to a real razor in the hands of a real barber, it was to find that my story had traveled forward and aft.

St. Paul was a very good man. He had piety and fervor, but also in a superior and godly fashion he was a man of the world. Perhaps he gained a firmer grip on his following by reason of his ability to say to the youth of his generation, "I have been twice stoned and thrice shipwrecked." I had been only once shipwrecked, yet a ready-made audience awaited entertainment.

It was on the second afternoon that Captain Keller appeared in the smoke-room. He was a man of about my own build and almost as bronzed, but fair haired and his carriage proclaimed the soldier before he introduced himself. I was idly enjoying the comfort of wicker chairs and windows which framed white decks and dancing seas. The few other occupants of the place were lounging about in pongee and linen, chatting lazily of those things which make talk among men coming out of the East: tribal risings in Java, the late race-meet in Melbourne. The military-looking young man dropped into a seat at my table and signaled to the spotless Jap, who officiated as smoking-room steward.

"Left you alone yesterday," he began by way of introduction. "I saw you didn't relish being treated like the newest and strangest animal in captivity. I guess they're accustomed to you now. What will you have?"

"Brandy and soda," I decided; then I added, "Perhaps after being rescued I ought to make myself more volatile and amusing, but the fact is I'm readjusting. Did you ever happen to spend six months on an undiscovered, cannibal island?"

He shook his head and laughed with a pleasant gleam of strong, regular teeth.

"Then," I assured him, "you don't understand the desire to sit still for a while. You don't understand the sheer wonder of a soft chair, white woodwork and the regular throb of engines and the sight of white-skinned, white-clad men and women. Look there." I held out my copper-colored forearm.

He smiled again and nodded. "I'm going back to the States," he said, "after three years in the Islands, capped with two months in India and Australia. I'm Keller of the 23rd Infantry."

He paused, then went on in a matter-of-fact way. "I've been in the jungle three months on end. I know what it means. This is my second term of Philippine service and it's the first time I've gone home quite sane. After the first three years the melancholia had me. When the transport left Manila, and I thought of the three weeks before I could see the Golden Gate, it took three good huskies to keep me from jumping overboard. It touches one here." With a finger at the temple, he paused, then added gravely: "And I know some fellows who weren't stopped in time. One must readjust slowly."

I nodded, puffing with a sense of supreme luxury at the Cairene cigarette he had offered me, and listening to the tinkle of ice in my tall glass.

There were some days of almost pure creature contentment and as we sat under deck awnings or burned cigars in the smoking-room our acquaintanceship ripened to intimacy. The engines with their muffled throb were churning out their fifteen knots an hour and the timbers creaked their complaint to the rise and fall of the prow. Of course all the time during those days was not spent chatting with the infantryman, and of course the point of intimate confidence was not at once established between us. Indeed, I, at first, let him do the talking, and though he was a modest man he had much to tell. But in the hours I spent alone I found my thoughts revolving about many things which I could not generally share. A man may admit to himself without shame that he has fallen in love with a woman of whose very existence he is uncertain, but he hesitates to announce it to another. Now, although the picture which had given me companionship and protection was packed away out of sight; though I was no longer a dweller in fantastic surroundings, I still had that presence with me. Whenever I closed my eyes I saw again the smiling lips and gracious eyes. I knew that I was henceforth destined to scan all faces until I found hers.

So, being unable to discuss matters that were distracting me I found need of an outlet, and sought it in transcribing this diary. Of course the impulse that had stirred me on the island to write down my emotions each day was one I could no longer gratify. Now I must do the thing in retrospect and my pen would lack the force which an impending shadow of fatality might have given it. I had emerged from that pall only to pass into the shadow of something quite as important. I was dedicated to a quest. When I found Her I wished to have the story ready to present in as convincing a form as possible. Sometimes at night Keller and I hung elbow to elbow over the after-rail, watching the broken phosphorus of the wake.

We were standing so on the night before reaching Honolulu where Keller was to spend a few days while I made immediate connection for the States. He was telling me many things about himself. There was a baby, born after he had left God's country, now old enough to chatter, and do wonderful things, whom he was to see for the first time when he reached 'Frisco. His confidence invited mine, and over our pipes, I told him the whole and true story of my experiences and of how an unknown goddess had safeguarded me.

"You spoke of the loneliness," I said at the end. "You know now why it didn't slug me into insanity."

For a long time he stood musing over the recital. He had seen enough of life's grotesqueries to understand it. Finally he asked:

"Will you read me some of your diary?"

I took him to my cabin and for an hour he listened while I read the hastily scrawled pages that I had set down. Of course I read them with a certain diffidence because it had occurred to me that certain phases might strike a man living in civilization as the vagaries of a brain touched with sun and isolation. Indeed, I was surreptitiously watching his face from time to time as a man might watch a jury box when he is on trial for lunacy, but I was reassured to find there no politely veiled judgment against my sanity.

"It's decidedly interesting," he said at last, "though it's one of the things we would rule out as too improbable to believe if we didn't happen to know it was true. In the first place I have been reliably informed by many expert witnesses that the South Seas have long since given up their last secrets as to undiscovered islands."

"I was also convinced of that," I admitted, "until I was cast up on one. I am now prepared to believe there are many others. Whenever I live six months in a place I am ready to admit its existence."

He refilled and lighted his pipe, then he said, "I don't want to invade private precincts, but after hearing that I'd like to see the portrait. May I?"

I delved into the mate's chest, and unwrapped the newspaper page.

For some moments he gazed at it, and I began to wonder whether it held the same magic infatuation for every one else that it did for me. His expression was enigmatical and his voice, when he spoke at last, was puzzled.

"It's very hackneyed," he said, "but we must go on saying it. The world is an extremely small place."

"What do you mean?" I demanded.

He was still looking at the picture and he spoke reflectively as though I had not been present.

"The loveliest girl in Dixie. They all said so."

"In Dixie," I echoed eagerly, "Do you mean you know her?"

"I've danced with her a dozen times," he answered, "and yet I can't say I know her. I remember that all the men were paying court, and I fancy I should have been smitten like the rest except that my wife had just accepted me, and I had only one pair of eyes."

"For God's sake," I said very quietly, "let me have all that you know about her—name—address."

"It was four years ago," he explained. "We were all at Bar Harbor. She was visiting at one of the cottages there. I was so engrossed with my own courtship that other girls, even this wonderful one, didn't count with me. I don't know where she lived, except that she was from the South. Her name was Frances." He broke off and an expression of extreme vexation clouded his face.

"I know her first name," I urged him. "It's the surname I need."

"Yes," he responded, "of course. Her surname was——" Again he halted and an embarrassed flush spread over his cheeks and forehead. Then he spoke impulsively. "You must bear with me. It's ludicrous, but the name has slipped me. It's just at the tip of my tongue, yet I can't call it. This thing is inexcusable, but ever since that first trip to the Islands I've been subject to it. Names which I know perfectly, elude me—sometimes for a few moments, sometimes for weeks."

"Can't you remember it," I demanded insistently, "if you cudgel your brain? I don't care how mercilessly you cudgel it. I must know."

He nodded. "I quite understand. It has slipped me. I shall remember it by morning, but—" his voice became graver.

"But what?" I inquired.

"I'm afraid it's too late to help you. We heard just before leaving the place that she was to marry some man at home. It hadn't been formally announced, but I think it was quite definite."

I suppose he said good-night and that I replied. I don't remember his leaving the stateroom. I recall standing some time later alone on the deck and seeing a white-clad officer tramping the bridge. His noiseless feet seemed to be treading upon me. The one honeymoon couple on our passenger-list passed and halted to comment on the rare quality of the air and the splendid softness of the stars. The little bride laughed delightedly. "Oh, Mr. Deprayne," she enthused, "it was under skies like this that Stevenson wrote,

"'The world is so full of a number of things,That I feel we should all be as happy as kings.'"

I smiled. "Yes," I murmured, "a number of things. Possibly too many things."

There was running through my memory a passage from the diary written by the unknown girl. It was one of those passages that had stuck in my memory through the shipwreck and the island days, a note of optimism which I had liked, partly because it was rather too imaginative to be accepted as fact. Now it mocked me.

"It's not just to-day's wonderful things that make life fair," she had written, "but it's knowing that there is to be a to-morrow, and that that same to-morrow will be lovelier than to-day. I know (I can't say why unless it's just that some voice keeps singing it to my heart), that some day he will come walking into my life as into a place where he has the right to be and our lives will after that be one life. That is the to-morrow I am waiting for."

---

# CHAPTER XIV

## THE "ASH-TRASH LADY"

But when we parted at Honolulu the name was still eluding Keller's memory and I had to continue on my way uninformed.

I was at first all for breaking my journey and remaining with him until some flash of memory should bring back the one word I needed, but he pointed out to me that little would be gained by this course. I think he was, in fact, so sensitive as to the mental quirk which had survived his attack that the idea of a man's shadowing him, waiting for him to remember, was unwelcome and would have taxed his self-respect. I felt bound to regard his whim, inasmuch as he promised that if I would wait a while, two or three weeks at the most, he would arm me with information. Even if his memory continued to play truant, a word with his wife, when he met her, would set him straight, and he would at once communicate with me.

At all events, as we shook hands, looking out across the sapphire bay, we both pretended that the lapse of his memory was a trivial thing. I did not affect indifference for its subject, but I assured him that inasmuch as I had still some days of voyage ahead of me it was quite probable that the name might come to his memory again before I landed in 'Frisco, and I made him promise that if such was the case he would cable the important surname to the St. Francis. There was still the bare chance, he reminded me, that the rumored engagement had not after all resulted in marriage. He fell back on those adages calculated to convey last hope to the forlorn, and since there was nothing else to be done I accepted his lame comfort in the spirit that prompted it. Possibly now that I had before me the prospect of learning the identity of the lady I really welcomed a few days of uncertainty. At least while they lasted I should have the shred of possible hope and could be shaping my resolution to face the answer. Long after one has told himself that there is no longer a chance of hope he none the less clings to a shred, and when I arrived at the hotel St. Francis and inquired for a cablegram, I think that relief outweighed disappointment as the clerk ran through the miscellaneous sheaf of messages and shook his head. "I don't find anything," he said, and strange as it may seem, I felt like a reprieved man who still faces dreaded news but has not actually received it.

Before that breakfast at the club my life had been merely prefatory; a sum of dilute emotions. At Harvard I had taken my degree and won my "H" on the gridiron. Since then I had gone through my days just missing every goal.

There had been little even of innocuous flirtation and nothing of grand passion.

I had tried to paint, and my masters discovered promise which came to nothing. I adventured into the practise of law and went briefless. I essayed music without distinction. I finally decided that my genius was seeking its goal along mistaken avenues. It should be mine to move men and women to smiles and tears by the magic of pen and ink and printed word. But the editors were on duty. They received my assaults on a phalanx of blue pencils. They flung me back, defeated and unpublished.

Perhaps had I fallen in love, it might have been different. Had some woman kindled the sleeping fires in me I might not have remained an extinct volcano of a man. Perhaps, so energized, I might have incited juries to tears—and verdicts. Possibly I might have stormed the editorial outposts and set my banner of manuscript at the forefront of literature. Be that as it may, I had heretofore never loved.

Now I did. Now I was the most quaintly tortured of men; wholly, unqualifiedly and to the depths, stirred by the worship of a woman I had never seen. Moreover she was probably some other man's wife and the mother of his children.

She had come to me over the sea, bringing with her my destiny. She had smiled on me and saved me. She had taken tribute of my soul. Now it was ended. I had worshiped her among crags of coral, under the dome of a volcano. I had come to think of her as a splendid and vivid orchid which a man might hope to wear very proudly at the heart of his life. To what end had the Fates lured me into this cul-de-sac?

I made the rest of the journey in a fog of sullen misery, and emerged, at its end, from the Pennsylvania station a morose and hopeless man. As a taxicab bore me to my club I felt a tremendous suspense. Doubtless there was a message there. If Keller's memory had flashed back to him, as memory sometimes does, the name in which I was so vitally interested, information should have arrived before me in New York. Since it had not intercepted me in San Francisco I judged that the blank had not, up to that time been filled. Supposing that he had remained in Hawaii a week, he would have left there a day after I arrived in 'Frisco, and then for the six days at sea I should hardly expect him to communicate with me. But I had stopped two days in the coast city, arranging financial affairs by telegraph, since I had landed stripped of everything but my chest and my borrowed clothes.

I had also crossed the continent, and by this time he should also have arrived in the States, unless his sailing had been again delayed. Of course I recognized that he had many things close to his own heart, but this service to me involved only the asking of a single question, which his wife could answer in one word. I was sure that he would not prove laggard in the matter, and so I braced myself at the door of the Club to receive tidings which might put hope to death, or might by bare possibility, give it new life.

And yet my mail held only the accumulation of unimportant things. Old advertisements and invitations and bills, many of which had come while I was out there at the edge of things.

Could it be, I asked myself, that Keller had forgotten me, too? Had it been possible that the card upon which I had so carefully written my address had been misplaced? I had been willing to put off the moment at San Francisco. Now I found myself eagerly impatient for the answer.

In the breakfast-room I encountered the doctor, who was dallying over a cup of coffee and a morning paper. He glanced up and for a moment his eyes lingered.

"Hello," he said, "how long have you been gone?"

"Little less than a year."

"You went away a youngish sort of man and you return with distinguished white temples." He summarized. "There must be a story locked up in you."

I glanced impatiently at the card and called for eggs.

"I haven't been nibbling at life this time," I retorted with some touch of asperity.

"I didn't instruct you to gluttonize," he reminded me.

I gave him only a partial history. Even the revised version of my adventures, which I had by this time learned to tell glibly enough to conceal the fact that I was omitting the major part, was sufficiently beyond the rut of things to beguile a half-hour in the eventless walls of a Manhattan club. But my table-companion eyed me with his customary and disquieting sharpness, and finally fell into his old habit of diagnosis.

"Something is lying heavily on your mind, Deprayne," he announced, "and it's not merely the memory of cannibals and exposure. Dangers of that sort become pleasant reminiscences when we view them through the retrospective end of the glasses. There's something else. What is it?"

I laughed at him over my raised coffee-cup. This was one man above all others in whom I should not confide the facts. He would promptly have prescribed a sanatorium.

"Nonsense!" I scoffed, and just as I said it a bell-boy arrived at the table with a telegram on a small silver tray.

"A message for Mr. Deprayne."

I was totally unable to control the violent start that caused the cup to drop on the tablecloth with a crash, and doubtless made my face momentarily pale. My effort at regained composure did not escape the doctor. I saw his eyes narrow and heard him murmur, "Nerves. Shaken nerves."

I took the telegram, calmly enough. I had had my moment of excitement and was again calm. I even held the missive unopened as the dining-room boys spread a clean napkin over the coffee stains. Then with a murmur of apology I tore the end and drew out the blank. I don't think the doctor detected the disgust of perusal.

"Have just arrived from Florida. If in town call and see me. Aunt Sarah."

Aunt Sarah was one of those disquieting persons who loathe telephones and note-paper. Her city messages came by wire with the insistence of commands.

The end was that the doctor decided I must get my mind active, and after vainly trying to bully me back into literary effort he took a new tack.

"Are you too surly and apathetic to combine a small service to friends with the augmenting of your own fortunes?" he demanded, and before I could reply he fell into the discussion of a matter which just now lay at the front of his interests. There was a Kentuckian in town, with glowing projects for fortune reaping along the ridges of the Cumberlands. He was not a mere promoter, but a man of large means and ability, who was also much the gentleman. His present scheme of things required the enlistment of additional capital, and he had come to men who had interested the doctor as well as themselves. The Kentuckian had suggested, however, that before committing themselves in the matter they send one of their own number with him to look over the options. None of the others, as it happened, could go. Here, declared the doctor, was my opportunity to try the novelty of useful occupation.

The man, whose name was Weighborne, was to lunch with him. Would I meet him and talk it over, and if I was favorably impressed accompany him to the Kentucky mountains?

We were sitting by a Fifth Avenue window as he outlined the matter with persuasiveness. The sky was drear with the ash gray of autumn. 'Busses, motors and taxis were trailing along in the same old hopeless monotony. At the thought of remaining here I sickened. Until a letter or message could arrive from Keller I could do little, and this trip would take only ten days or two weeks. I now inferred that Keller had awaited the next steamer. If that were so there would still be the six days at sea. At all events Kentucky is on the telegraph lines. His word could follow me there without loss of time. Then he had said, "the loveliest girl in Dixie." South of Mason and Dixon's line I might be closer to my discoveries when the name arrived. But above all that, I must fill in the time of waiting with some sort of action. There in the hills I should at least be away from the scenes which, in the few hours since my return, had begun to spell insufferable *ennui*. Yes, I said I would meet Mr. Weighborne. Why not?

Having promised to be on hand at two o'clock, I began a strange quest that came to nothing. In Times Square and Park Row I spent several dusty hours running through newspaper files, and going back to dates five and six years old. I was hunting for a pictorial section of the same general style as that which bore the portrait. I found one or two printed with a like make-up on similar paper, but not even of the exact size, and although I followed these through the Sundays of several years, I came in the end only to the conclusion that the paper had been printed outside of New York.

Weighborne impressed me. In physique and mind and energy he was big and virile. One could glance at him in his carelessly correct clothes and know that he would be equally at home in drawing-room or saddle. The Kentuckian had to cut short his visit with us, since he was leaving the same day for the South, and what talk we had was limited in its scope. Yet his personality charmed me and compelled admiration. He was that type of man who escaped the preliminaries with which the average promoter of large schemes must convince his hearers. His own bearing and breadth carried with it an assurance of trustworthiness and energy. His steady gray eyes had a compelling and purposeful clarity, and I could not help thinking as we talked what such a companionship would have meant in those other days of loneliness and danger. Weighborne was the sort of fellow one would like to have at his back in difficulties. I agreed to meet him in Lexington three days hence and accompany him to the properties which he hoped to develop.

There was a minor element of personal risk, he warned me. We should perhaps encounter the dislike of certain men who were of the feudist type. He spoke lightly of this feature, but as a matter concerning which it was only the part of fairness to inform me.

Later in the day while glancing over the papers I came upon the announcement that a new play was to have its première that evening at a Broadway house, and in the name of the author, I found my interest piqued. Bob Maxwell was an old friend. He had fought a long fight for success and had found the goddess cold and offstanding. We had been fellows in literary aspiration, and he had been, when I last saw him, still floundering for support in the unstable waters of newspaperdom. If his play succeeded, he was made. I tried vainly to reach him by 'phone, and went that evening to the theater to lend my applause.

From the unpainted side of the stage-sets I listened to the salvoes of handclapping that were waves lifting him to success.

When at last the ordeal was over and my friend's triumph assured, he led me along the whitewashed walls to the star's dressing room. In response to his rapping, the door opened on a scene of confusion. The young woman whom the coming of this night had made a star turned upon us, from her make-up mirror, a triumphantly flushed face.

The place was aglow with elation. The spirit of success showed even in the movements of the quiet little French maid as she gathered and stored the beribboned linen which still littered the green-room. Grace Bristol herself took a quick, impulsive step forward and placed a grateful hand on each of the author's shoulders. For me, when I was presented, she had only a hurried nod of greeting.

"Thank God, Bobby!" she exclaimed with a half-hysterical catch in her throat. "Thank God, it's over. My knees were knocking so while I was waiting for my entrance cue that I wanted to run away and hide."

"I know," he said. "I was watching you. You were green under the paint, Grace."

"If you'd spoken to me just then, I'd have screamed and had spasms," she laughed, "but now—" she pointed victoriously to a maze of roses on her dresser—"there are the flowers that glow under glass, tra-la! You wrote me the bulliest part I ever played, old pal. You made me a star." I had come to-night simply to congratulate. I had known something of my friend's struggles and I wished to be among those who were there to say "well done." My own thoughts were coursing in channels far away from the life of theaters and green-rooms, where this young woman, undeniably pretty, beyond doubt talented, was enjoying her moment of high triumph. In her delight was that hysterical touch which stamps moments of reaction. She had been through the ordeal of a "first night" and now she knew that the experiment was successful. Bobby too must have had the same exaltation, though his masculine nature did not break so frankly into emotion. I felt that I was the extra person, entirely superfluous, so I murmured some good-night and started to leave the place. But my friend stopped me.

"I want to talk with you later, old man," he said, and I remained to be, as it developed, catapulted into a new discovery.

Bobby helped Miss Bristol into her coat and the two of us gathered up as many of the flowers as we could carry and made our way with her through the stage-entrance and out into the street. As we hailed a taxi' at the curb, the night life of never-sleeping places was racing at full tide along Broadway, and swirling in an eddy about Longacre Square. It bore on its crest its gay flotillas of pleasure—and its drift of derelicts. To me it pointed all the miserable morals of contrast.

"Where to?" inquired Bobby. "Do you show yourself in triumph at Rector's grill, or go home to dream of applauding thousands?"

The lady shrugged her shapely shoulders.

"Me for the hay!" she announced with prompt decisiveness. "Jump in, boys," she invited in afterthought. "I may as well drive you down to your rooms and drop you first. I need a breath of air to quiet my nerves."

Out of the garish color and clangor of Broadway, we swept into the tempered quiet of Fifth Avenue, stretching ghostlike between the twin threads of electric opals.

"We must both be pretty tired," he suggested when Washington Arch loomed ahead. "We haven't spoken since Herald Square."

"I'm too happy to talk," she answered. "For ten pretty rough years I've been building for to-night." She sighed contentedly, then went on, "I began about the usual way ... musical comedy ... in tights ... carrying a spear. My first promotion was to the front row. I wasn't fool enough to kid myself into the notion that it was because I was a Melba or a Fiske. If I used to go to my hall bedroom every night and cry myself to sleep it was nobody's business but my own." She must have felt Maxwell's eyes on her, for her voice took on a note of the defiant as she added, "And if I didn't always go straight to my hall bedroom, maybe that was my own business too." She seemed to be reviewing her struggle as she leaned restfully back against the cushions with to-night's roses in her lap. Her lids drooped contentedly. "But to-night," she added, "well, to-night I felt all that was paid for and the receipt signed. How do you feel, Bobby?"

"Glad it's over," said the man. "I'm tired."

"It hasn't been just exactly a snap for you either," she sympathetically conceded. "When I first knew you, you were haunting Park Row for a cheap job, and getting canned by office boys. It's been a long way, we've come, boy, but we kept plugging when the going was bad, and now, thank God, we've arrived."

The taxi' drew up before the door of the house where Maxwell had his quarters. It was a dingy building which has harbored under its roof the beginnings of a half-dozen literary reputations.

"Bobby," said the young woman suddenly, "have you any Scotch in your rooms?"

He reflected.

"I believe there's some Bourbon left in the bottle," he admitted.

"'Twill have to do," she said with a grimace. "I believe I'll climb the steps and have a highball. We ought to toast the piece, you know. It's been good to us."

"I thought you were too tired," suggested the author in surprise. "We might have stopped where they had champagne."

"I didn't want wine. But I need a quiet little chat to work off this nervousness."

In his sitting-room Bobby announced, "I've got to pack. I'm leaving in the morning. Deprayne will entertain you with traveler's tales."

Miss Bristol paused with her hands raised and her hatpins half drawn. Her face, for a moment, clouded.

"Where are you going?"

"Out west for a month or two."

"Oh," she said slowly. "What's the idea? Girl?"

He shook his head.

"Rest," he enlightened. "I'm tired."

The smile came again to her lips.

"Oh, very well," she said. "Get out your bag. I'll help you pack it."

Maxwell went in search of glasses and bottles.

A shaded lamp on the table left the corners of the book-lined walls in shadow. In the open fireplace a bank of coals glowed redly. The young woman took her place before it on the Spanish-leather cushions of a divan, drawing her feet under her and nestling snugly back with her hands clasped behind her head. Her lips were parted in a smile and her eyes, fixed on the coals, were deep with reflection. The face became again the face of a young girl, bearing no trace of the experience which had made up ten years of war with Broadway. To me she paid not the slighted attention. Shortly he returned and handed us glasses. She raised hers, smiling.

"To you," she said—"the author!"

They clinked rims.

"To you," he gravely responded,—"the star!"

After that neither of them spoke, until the girl broke the silence with a laugh.

"Some day, Bobby" she asserted, "you must tell me the story you haven't dramatized—the story of your life."

"Why do you think it would prove interesting?"

She regarded him for a time with close scrutiny.

"Well, I don't quite get you, Bobby. You are rather a riddle in a way. Sir Galahad on Broadway—doesn't that strike you as a funny combination?"

"Rather paradoxical," he admitted, "the environment might fit Don Juan better. But why Sir Galahad on Broadway?"

"That's what they all call you. You are notoriously unattainable. The only man in this game who hasn't had an affair with any ash-trash."

"With any what?" he questioned, puzzled.

"Ash-trash; actress," she enlightened. "The title is a little conceit of my own—poor but original. You know perfectly well that Stella Marcine simply threw herself at your head during the rehearsals. And she told me that you never even asked her out to supper."

"Why should I?"

She smiled.

"Everybody else does. Most men marry her, at one time or another."

"Oh."

"Of course," she went on thoughtfully after a pause, "it's very charming to remain naïve after years of this life, unless, as stage gossip says, it's merely a pose."

"It's not a pose," replied the man quietly.

"I know that," she hastened to assure him. "But what I want to know is this. What's behind it? Who is she?"

"Why should there necessarily be any She?" he demanded. "Can't a man live his own life independently of prevalent customs—merely because it is his own life?"

She shook her head and flecked the ash from her cigarette. She seemed to be pondering the matter before hazarding judgment. Then her words came positively enough.

"Don't pull that old line on me, about being the captain of your soul, Bobby; I know better.... Oh, I used to believe all those pretty things. I wanted to go on believing them, but there wasn't a chance."

"What did you find?"

"Just what the fool sailor finds who has the idea that he's bigger than tides and gales; who fancies he can sail his little duck-pond boat in the gulf stream, through reefs and hurricanes and bring it out with the paint fresh." Her voice had perceptibly hardened. "You probably know a lot of girls, Bobby, who wouldn't invite me to tea—certainly not if they knew all my story. Nevertheless when we line up for the big tryout, I guess the Almighty will take a look at their untempted innocence, and a glance at me—and somehow I'm not worried about what He'll say. No woman would muddy her shoes if we all had Walter Raleighs to spread coats over the puddles."

The man lighted a cigarette and said nothing.

"But get the angle on me right, Bobby," she hastened to amend. "I haven't loafed. Now, I've made good. From this on I *can* be the captain of my soul—and you can be pretty sure I will."

---

# CHAPTER XV

## TWO DISCOVERIES

Bob Maxwell was standing before the fire. He turned abstractedly and set his untouched glass on the mantel shelf.

"You've got a grouch, Bobby," lectured the young actress, "at a time when you ought to be all puffed up and chesty. Aren't you glad we made good in the same piece? It would be nice of you to say so."

He turned on her a face strangely drawn and his words came swiftly in agitation.

"Triumph, did you say? Don't you know that it's only when you get the thing you've worked for, that you realize it's not worth working for? That's not triumph—it's despair. Triumph means laying your prize at somebody's feet—" he broke off with a sort of groan. "To hell with such success!" he burst out with sudden bitterness. "To hell and damnation with the whole of it!"

For a long while the girl held him in a steady scrutiny. They had both forgotten me, silent in my corner. Her cheeks paled a little, and when finally she reiterated her old question, her steady voice betrayed the training of strong effort.

"Who is she?"

"Listen, Grace," he said. "I've got to talk to some one. You have come here, so you let yourself in for it.... Ten years ago I was reporting on a paper for a few dollars a week. It was a long way from Broadway. There was a dusty typewriter and dirty walls decorated with yellowed clippings—but ... There was wild young ambition and all of life ahead. *That* was living."

"Who was she?" insistently repeated the actress, when he paused.

"What can it matter how big a play one writes," demanded the author, "if he presents it to an empty house? The absence of one woman can make any house empty for any man. I'd give it all, to hear her say once more—" He broke off in abrupt silence.

"To hear her say what, Bobby?" prompted Grace Bristol, softly.

"Well," he answered with a miserable laugh, "something she used to say."

"I suppose, Bobby—" the girl spoke very slowly, and a little wistfully, too—"I suppose it wouldn't do any good to—to hear any one else say it?"

He shook his head.

"Do you remember, Grace," he went on, "the other evening, when we were sitting in the café at the Lorillard and the orchestra in another room was playing 'Whispering Angels'? The hundred noises of the place almost drowned it out, yet we were always straining our ears to catch the music— and when there came a momentary lull, it would swell up over everything else. That's how it is with this—and sometimes it swells up and slugs one— simply slugs one, that's all." He broke off and laughed again. "I guess I'm talking no end of rot. You probably don't understand."

She raised her face and spoke with dignity.

"Why don't I understand, Bobby? Because I'm a show-girl?"

My old friend's voice was contrite in its quick apology.

"Forgive me, Grace—of course I didn't mean that. You're the cleverest woman on Broadway."

She laughed. "I'm said to be quite an emotional ash-trash," she responded.

It seemed inconceivable that Maxwell should miss the note of bitter misery in her voice; yet, blinded by his own quarrel with Fate, he passed into the next room oblivious of all else.

She crossed to the table which lay littered with the confusion of his untidy packing, and took up a shirt that he had left tumbled. She carefully folded it, then with a surreptitious glance over her shoulder to make sure that she was not observed, she tore a rose from her belt and, holding it for an impulsive moment against her breast, dropped it into the bag. My face was averted, but through a mirror I saw the pitiful pantomime. From the table she turned and stood gazing off through his window, with her face averted. From my seat I could also catch some of the detail that the window framed. Below stretched Washington Square, almost as desolately empty as in those days when, instead of asphalt and trees and fountain, it held only the many graves of the pauper dead. The arch at the Avenue loomed stark and white and the naked branches of a sycamore were like skeleton fingers against the garish light flung from an arc lamp. The girl had thrown up the sash and stood drinking in the cold air, though she shivered a little, and forgetful of my presence clenched her hands at her back.

From the bedroom, to which Bobby had withdrawn, drifted his voice in the melancholy tune and words of one of Lawrence Hope's lyrics:

"Less than the dust beneath thy chariot wheels—"

The girl at the window turned with a violent start and her exclamation broke passionately from lips, for the moment trembling.

"For God's sake, Bobby, *don't*!"

"What's the matter with my singing?" demanded his aggrieved voice from beyond the door.

She forced a laugh.

"Oh, nothing," she said carelessly enough, "only when anybody pulls one of those Indian Love Lyrics on me, I pass."

He returned a moment later to find her still standing by the window. At last she turned back to the room and took up her hat. She lifted it to her head as though it were very heavy, and her arms very tired.

"I guess, Bobby, I'll be running along," she announced.

"Grace," he said earnestly, "it's good to know that from this time on you are a star."

She laughed.

"Yes, isn't it?" she answered. "I'm a real ash-trash now. No—don't bother to see me down. Mr. Deprayne will put me into the taxi'."

Outside the threshold she paused to thrust her head back into the room, and to laugh gaily as she shouted in the slang of the street:

"Oh, you Galahad!"

But her eyes were swimming with tears.

As I climbed the creaking stairs again, I was pondering the question of contentment. Here were three of us. One had raked success out of the fire of failure and had written what promised to be the season's dramatic sensation. One had earned the right to read her name, nightly, in Broadway's incandescent roster. I myself had been preserved from cannibal flesh-pots. All of us were seemingly brands snatched from the burning, and all of us were deeply miserable. I wondered if the fourth was happy; the woman who had once said to Maxwell the things he now vainly longed to hear? And She—the lady I had never seen; what of her?

I found the author gazing off with a far-away reminiscence which was mostly pain. The taxi' was whirring under the arch, but he had already forgotten it and its occupant.

"Do you want to unbosom yourself, Bobby?" I questioned.

He shook his head.

"To you?" he inquired with a smile. "You're a woman-hater."

But a moment later he came over and laid his hand affectionately on my shoulder, fearing he had offended me.

"I guess, old man," he explained, "there's no balm in post-mortems. I loved her, that's all, and I still do."

"She married?" I inquired.

"She is now Mrs. William Clay Weighborne of Lexington. It's a prettier name than Fanny Maxwell, and looks better on a check. I was number three, that's all."

"Mrs. Who?" I repeated, in astonishment. "You don't mean the wife of W. C. Weighborne?"

"Why?" he asked suddenly. "Is the gentleman an acquaintance of yours?"

"Since this morning, yes. He is even a business associate."

"How you birds of a financial feather do flock around the same pabulum," he coolly observed.

"I was rather well impressed with him," I admitted idiotically enough. "He seemed a very decent sort of chap."

Maxwell lighted a cigarette. His voice was a trifle unenthusiastic as he replied.

"So I am informed."

A few days later I arrived at Lexington and Weighborne, who met me at the station with his car, announced that I was to go to his home on the Frankfort turnpike. But at this arrangement I balked. Despite a certain curiosity to see his wife, the lady who had left such a melancholy impress on the heart of my friend, there were considerations which outweighed curiosity. My own peculiar afflictions bore more heavily on me than those of my acquaintances and I had no yearning for the effort of socializing.

So Weighborne protestingly drove me to the Ph[oe]nix, and armed me with a visitor's card to the Lexington Union Club. I could see that he was deeply absorbed. His mind was so tensely focused on coal and timber development that it was difficult for him to think of other matters. My apathy lagged at the prospect of following his untiring energy over hours of close application to detail. I would put it off until to-morrow. Yet I had hardly taken my seat at table in the dining-room of the Ph[oe]nix, when a page called me to the telephone booth and Weighborne's voice came through the transmitter.

"Hullo, old man, did I drag you away from food? Sorry, but there are some papers here I'd like mighty well to have you look over. I might bring them in, but if you don't mind running out it would be better."

Of necessity I assented.

"I'll have my chauffeur call for you at 8:30," he arranged, "and meanwhile I'll be getting things into shape here. By the way"—his voice took on a reassuring note—"you sidestepped my rooftree this evening, and I gathered that you were not in the mood for meeting people."

I murmured some insincere assurance to the contrary, which did not beguile him.

"We shall have the house quite to ourselves," he said. "All the family are flitting off to a dance at the Country Club."

An hour later his car turned in at a stone gate, and up a long maple-lined avenue. From the windows of a generously broad, colonial mansion came a cheery blaze of light, throwing shadows outward from the tall white columns at the front. I could not help thinking of Maxwell's lodgings in Washington Square, and reflecting that, all prejudice aside, the flower of his worship had not chosen so badly in transplanting herself here.

Weighborne met me at the entrance of a hall over which hung the charm of ripe old portraits and wainscoted walls. Furnishings of unostentatious elegance made the place a delight. We passed into a large library where a wide hearth dispensed the cheer of blazing logs and our feet sunk deep in Persian rugs.

Yet even here, although instinctively hospitable, my host was plainly immersed in thoughts of coal and timber, for as soon as he had done the honors he plunged me into a litter of statistics.

I, poor business man that I was, had, time after time, to force my mind back from its undisciplined straying. As he talked of coal veins, I would find myself thinking of coral reefs. When he enlarged upon advances in timber tracts I would be seeing in my memory a circle of mahogany-skinned pigmies squatting silently about a portrait spiked to a sailor's chest with a pair of Damascus daggers.

At last Weighborne began sorting through the papers for some misplaced and necessary memorandum. He crossed the room to a desk at one corner which he found locked, and his ejaculation was one of deep annoyance.

"My wife has locked the desk and Heaven only knows where she has put the key," he complained. "I'll have to call the Country Club and ask her."

His words must have carried to the next room, for at once a voice answered. It was a richly musical contralto, and at its first syllable my heart stood still, and the room commenced to whirl about me. I had never heard it and yet I *had* heard it—singing in a wilderness of coral and orchids. Surely after all the big, little doctor was right, I was becoming a lunatic.

"Billy," called the voice, "you needn't 'phone. I'm here. I'll unlock it."

My host turned in surprise and walked over to the door.

"Hullo, Frances!" he exclaimed. "Didn't you go to the Club?"

"I had a headache," replied the voice. "I sent the others off, and stayed at home. I'll come in just a moment."

I stood waiting, my pulses pounding turbulently. Had my host not been just then dedicated to a single idea he must have noticed my pallor and wondered at the fascination with which I came to my feet and stood gazing at the door.

And as I gazed she appeared on the threshold, the blaze from the logs lighting her and throwing a nimbus about her hair of gold and honey. I placed both my hands on the top of the table and braced myself as a man may do when the executioner whispers the warning "ready!"

She might have stepped from the picture herself. Again she was in evening dress, which clung to her in soft lines of unspeakable grace. At her throat hung a string of pearls—the same pearls—and as she paused and our eyes met, I could have sworn that her muscles grew momentarily taut, and her lips twitched in a gasp. She put out one hand and steadied herself against the door jamb; then with the gracious recognition of a half-smile for a guest not yet duly presented, she went over and unlocked the desk.

I stood looking after her. I was conscious of a numbness of spirit—a sickening of hopelessness. The question was answered. The Frances of my Island, the Frances of Maxwell's heartbreak, the Frances who had married my business associate, were, by a monstrous sequence of hideous circumstances and coincidence, one and the same. She stood ten feet and twenty sky depths away from me.

# CHAPTER XVI

## AN INTERVIEW AND A CRISIS

As I stood there all immediate things were apparitions seen vague and distorted through a chaos of wild emotion. I had assumed that for an experimenter in the unexpected I could qualify as tried and seasoned. Now it seemed that all prior assaults upon my equanimity had been mere kindergarten exercises in control.

Weighborne, still too self-absorbed to see that worlds were crumbling in his library, turned suddenly to us with an apologetic laugh.

"Frances," he said, "forgive me, I entirely forgot to present our guest." Even then he did not present me, but turned to me to add, "We've talked of you so much here, Mr. Deprayne, that I had overlooked the fact that introductions were in order. I'm the unfortunate type of one idea at a time. After all, I hope you'll feel that, having crossed the threshold you are one of us, and that further formalities may be dispensed with." Then as I bowed, somewhat incoherently mumbling my acknowledgments, he turned his back upon the room and busied himself again with the rubbish that claimed his interest at the desk.

I wanted to leap for his throat. I, who had presented her as a goddess to a people under skies that rose from the ocean and dipped again to the ocean, needed no presentation. The casual fashion of his amenities was in itself an affront.

Of course all this was insanely unfair to my host, and even while my thoughts seethed in this unamiable vortex—so strong is the grip of artificial conventions—I was attempting to smile with the agreeable inanity of a drawing-room smirk.

But as she stood there I could read in her face also the record of the strange agitation that had evidenced itself at the door. Her spirit too was in equinox. The lips I knew so well, though only in one expression, were now grave and a little drawn, and her eyes held a wild questioning, as though my coming brought a startling riddle.

In a moment she was again the perfectly poised mistress of herself. She came over and offered her hand and as I took it she met my eyes smiling, though she must have read in them the rising hunger of a man for a woman—a hunger which in me was so poignant that my soul was the soul of a wolf. The touch of her fingers electrified me and the tremor of my own hand, before I withdrew it, must have telegraphed whatever my pupils failed to mirror.

That wordless message told her how my sanity reeled on the brink of seizing her and holding her in wild defiance of this man, across the room, whose name she bore.

"I won't interrupt business," she was saying with perfect serenity. "But later I hope to see you again."

I bowed. "I hope so," I answered politely, while a wave of anger swept me.

She would not interrupt! She who had snapped all the thread of life and let my soul go plunging down the abysses.

She would not interrupt!

The grandfather clock against the wall stood at nine twenty-four. At nine twenty I had been stolidly puffing one of Weighborne's Havanas and listening to his disquisitions on courts of appeals decisions and squatters' rights. The cigar which I had dropped on an ash-tray at the first sound of her voice still held its ash and sent up a thin spiral of smoke. It had outlived me.

My host plunged afresh into his papers. He might as well have been reading me ukases from the Romonoff Czar in the undiluted Russian. But as the clock ticked off the half-hour I seemed to freeze out of the eruptive and into the glacial stage. I felt my lips drawing into a stiff smile. I even contrived to nod my head in sedulous and ape-like agreement when he raised interrogative eyes to mine. So rapidly had my volcanic lava of spirit hardened to clinkers that when the telephone called him to a barn, where some accident had befallen a thoroughbred colt, I was able to turn a conventionally masklike countenance on Frances, who came to chat with me till his return. She sat in a great leather chair, and I, standing on the hearth, looked down on her, braced for whatever might develop. I was resolved to make amends for my self-revelation of a half-hour ago; I should at least prove myself the capable mummer; yet I found that I was fettered by an unaccustomed silence.

There was only one topic on which I could find words for talk with this woman and that topic was forbidden. She, too, for some unaccountable reason, seemed hampered by a diffidence which her bearing told me was foreign to her normal nature. So, for a while, our conversation lagged and faltered and fell into fitful fragments and puerile tatters, while my gaze devoured her. There was no flaw in the perfection of her beauty from the coils of her amber and honey hair to the white satin toe of her small slipper. I had given opulent scope to my painter's fancy in those island days and had imagined her, in the color of life, as a being expressed in the souls of orchids. Now I realized, with a terrible yearning, that I had not done her justice.

Step by step I went back over the record of the last year and found it painfully distinct and clear. I had, with my imagination built a house of cards which had tottered. I had been lonely and morbid and had pretended a picture was a woman. It had come to mean a great deal—clay idols have come to mean immortal gods to poor creatures who have had no better deities. I had told myself that the finger of Destiny had traced through my life a thread of gold linking my life to hers. After all it had been nothing more than a series of inconceivable coincidences. I had no more part in her cosmos than in that of any woman whose photograph I might have admired in a miscellaneous collection. It behooved me to scourge out of my brain the mischievous chimeras I had harbored there. As for her momentary excitement—the something vague and deep and disturbed in her pupils as she stood at the door and later when we touched hands; that was only the psychic realization that this guest of her husband was staring at her out of insanely wild eyes.

I started to speak, then halted, perplexed over a ridiculous point. How should I address her? On the island I had called her Frances, and now I could no more compel my rebellious tongue to frame the title "Mrs. Weighborne" than I could have forced it to utter an epithet. So I said nothing at all.

"You are a great traveler, aren't you, Mr. Deprayne?" she suggested when the silence had begun to be oppressive.

---

**"You are a great traveler, aren't you, Mr. Deprayne?" she suggested when the silence had begun to be oppressive.**

---

I had always been accounted a talkative man. One could read in her face that she had the wit to sparkle in conversation like champagne in cut glass, yet under the constraint that had settled over us, we labored as platitudinously as a knickerbockered boy and a school-girl entertaining her first caller.

"I have traveled a little," I answered.

"And encountered unusual adventures?"

"No—just traveled."

"Billy says," she went on as graciously as though I had not rebuffed every conversational advance, "that you were shipwrecked in the south seas and wounded by savages."

"Billy!" My bruised consciousness flinched under the familiarity of the title and I fell back upon shameless churlishness.

"A nigger stuck me with a spear," I admitted shortly.

She glanced quickly up with perplexity. Her eyes seemed to read that I was not at heart a boor and her graciousness remained impervious to my ruffianism.

"I wish," she said slowly, "you would tell me about it, or are you one of the men who tell women only empty and pretty things?"

There was a vagrant hint of wistfulness in the tone of the question. I wondered if she had been fed, like the girl of our diary, too much on sweetmeats, and wanted a more nutritious fare.

"It wouldn't interest you," I apologized, melting at once to penitence. Then for a moment came a wild up-sweep of emotion. It was one of those impulses which master men and, when the trend is violent, make the eyes swim with blood and the hand rise to murder. With me it swept to sentiment, and carried me uncontrollably in its undertow.

"I wish," I said with an intensity which must have carried a note of wildness, "I wish to God I were back on that island now!"

The perplexed questioning of her eyes steadied me again into self-command.

"I crave your pardon," I said with a disingenuous laugh. "It's the call of the wild."

"Perhaps I understand something of that call," was her enigmatical reply.

I wondered. Could she understand? This woman with the perfect drawing-room poise; this creature of exquisite art? Even if I were absolutely free to tell her the whole story, from Suez to the Golden Gate, how much and how little would it mean to her? Could she comprehend a passion fired with no touch of the physical, painted horizon-wide against a canvas of cobalt sky? Perhaps not, but I wished as I had never wished any other thing that I might have been privileged to learn.

Her personality, even in silence, wove an aura of subtle magic about her. She wore at her breast several hot-house orchids. They were pale and exotic, quick wilting and artificial. Already the edges of their petals were curling and darkening. Was she like them? Could she have carried her splendid shoulders with the same grace through jungles and over mountains? Could she bloom with the wild splendor of those other orchids in the sterner environment of God's great out-of-doors?

She smiled as she questioned me.

"You are sceptical of my power to understand things, aren't you?"

"I was wondering," I answered, "just what you meant by it."

"I meant," she said slowly, as her eyes clouded again with that wistfulness which had a few moments before cost me my self-control, "that civilized women lead even narrower lives than civilized men. Maybe they feel even more strongly than men the longing for wider, freer things."

"But in these times," I inanely suggested, struggling to maintain the pretense of conversation, "woman has a full measure of liberty."

She tossed her head with an airy contempt for my reasoning and bent her eyes for a moment on the tip of her satin slipper. "About as much as a canary in a cage," she announced, "and we are expected to sing joyously for our cuttle bone and hemp seed. I wonder that it never seems to occur to you men that we women may want something more than that; that we may not be satisfied after all to hear affectionate things chirped through the cage wires—that even human canaries may be able to conceive of some horizon broader than a window-sill with a pot or two of geraniums to give it color."

I loved this woman. Why in all conscience did my heart leap almost triumphantly at the hint that she was restive in captivity? Was it merely because it was not I who was her captor? Was it jealousy feeding on the crumbs of a misery shared? There was a long silence.

She had been toying as she talked with a slender gold chain, and under an involuntary emphasis of her fingers it had given way. She was now trying to close the broken link with her teeth. I stepped forward and, without realizing that I was doing it, caught her hand in my restraining fingers. She looked up quickly.

"I beg your pardon," I said hastily, "but don't bite that with your teeth."

"If I bite it at all," she replied with impervious logic, "I must bite it with my teeth."

I took it from her and began the simple work of repair. The contact of my fingers had left me vibrating, and as I bent my face over the chain, my hands were trembling.

"Why," she demanded in a soft voice, leaning back and clasping her hands behind her head, "won't you tell me the story of your island?" Into the question crept a teasing note of whimsical insistence.

"Because," I answered, "there is a part of it which I couldn't tell you—and without that there is nothing to tell."

"Will you tell me some other time when you know me better?" she inquired as naively as a little girl, pleading for a favorite fairy tale.

At every turn she flashed a new angle of herself to view. At one moment she was impressively regal, at the next an appealing, coaxing child; at one instant her eyes hinted at heart-hunger and at the next her lips knew no curves but those of laughter.

And yet there was a thing about it all that hurt and disappointed me. With nothing tangible, there was still, in a subtle way, much which was sheer coquetry of eye and lip. It was invitation. Why did she challenge me to forbidden things so easy to say, so impossible to unsay? She must know that from the moment I saw her I had stood at a crisis; and that this was true only because I loved her. Such things need no words for their telling.

"I'm afraid I shall be denied the privilege of knowing you better," I said slowly, "I leave for the mountains to-morrow morning."

"You won't be there forever," she retorted, "sha'n't we see you on the return trip?"

I shook my head.

"I must hurry back East."

"I'm sorry," she answered with sweet graciousness. Any woman in the country houses about her would probably have spoken in the same fashion, but to me it was a match touched to powder.

"I will quote you a parable," I said, and although I attempted to smile, that the speech might be taken lightly, I had that rigid feeling about the lips and brow which made me conscious that my face was drawn and tell-tale.

"Icarus was the original bird-man, and he came to grief. His wings were fastened on with wax, but they worked fairly well until he soared too close to the sun. Then they melted ... and the first aviation disaster was chronicled."

She looked at me frankly and level-eyed, but her face held only mystification.

"I'm afraid," she said, "you must construe the parable."

I shook my head gravely. "I'm glad you don't take its meaning."

"I don't understand," she repeated, yet we both felt that we were standing in the presence of dammed-up emotions which might at any moment break over and inundate us. She might yet have no realization of it, but I knew by an occult assurance, in no way related to egotism, that I could make her love me. My fable was false after all. I had already fallen and been broken; my pinions were trailing and blood-stained. There was yet time to save her. During our silence Weighborne opened the door and our interview was ended.

It had lasted a few minutes, yet during their continuance I had been several times perilously near the brink. I saw her rise and smile and leave the room, and I caught or fancied I caught a glance from her eyes and a miraculous curve of her lips at the threshold. The expression was subtle and challenging, seeming to say to me, "You will tell me many things before I am through with you." Of course, that, too, was my disordered imagination, yet for the moment it was as though she had actually spoken words of self-confidence and conquest. And I knew that if I saw her again I should say many things—forbidden things. Resentment and bitterness and utter heartache possessed me, and I heard my host's voice in a maddeningly matter-of-fact pitch as he commented, "Now I hope our interruptions are over."

As I went to my room at the hotel that night a telegram was handed me. I did not at once open it. I presumed that it was from Keller, and it was all of a piece with my grotesque ill luck that the answer should come just after I had myself in the most painful possible way solved the problem. In my room, however, I read, under a San Francisco date, "Name Weighborne, not Carrington. Keller." It was evidently a telegraphic mistake and should have read "Weighborne née Carrington." Keller had told me who she had been before she married Weighborne, the man whose name, in the words of my fellow unfortunate, Bobby Maxwell, "looked well on a check."

---

# CHAPTER XVII

## WE GO TO THE MOUNTAINS.

Weighborne was at the station on the following morning when, five minutes before train time, I arrived. He was clad for his mountain environment in high lace boots, corduroy breeches and flannel shirt, and in this guise he loomed bigger and stronger of seeming than in conventional clothing. His level, straight-gazing eyes held the cheery satisfaction of facing, after a good breakfast, a prospect of action. He was meanwhile willing to fill the interim of railroad travel with conversation. I, on the contrary, knew that sleeplessness had left me haggard, and met his advances, I fear, with churlish taciturnity.

In the smoking compartment, when we were under way, I sat gazing out of the car window at fleeting fields still a-sparkle with frost crystals on wood and stubble.

"You and Frances didn't just seem to hit it off," commented my companion with a proffer of his cigar-case, "or rather Frances liked you all right, but you—" He broke off with an amused smile and busied himself with the kindling of a panatella.

A man can hardly explain to his fellow-man, "I was rude to your wife because I love her. I worship her in a way your prosaic little soul can never understand. It is only because civilization is all distorted that I don't murder you and carry her off in triumph to my cave—where she belongs."

So I mumbled some foolish contradiction. I thought her charming; I was merely not a woman's man. I was still part savage. My unfortunate temperament must be my apology.

Weighborne studied me for a moment in some perplexity. He knew I was lying, but he had no suspicion why I lied and he could hardly argue in her defense with me, a stranger. He changed the topic, but there was a hurt expression in his face as though he were unable to understand my subtle hostility, as he construed it, for a person entirely lovely. If I did not like Frances there must be something abnormal about me, and the expression was quite eloquent though wordless. I had no difficulty in reading it. It was as though he wanted to say to me and was saying to himself, "After all, our relations are those of business, and your personal preferences and prejudices do not concern me, but we won't speak of Her again. It shall be a prohibited topic between us." In this tacit attitude I found an element of relief. If I were to be forced into his daily companionship I must not be specifically reminded at every turn that he was the husband of his wife. I had stepped knee-deep into this miserable Rubicon of financial venture as the agent of others, and turning back was impossible. Afterward.... But at this point I stopped. I could not yet bring myself to think of any afterward.

Inasmuch as Weighborne and I were for a time to travel the same trail and since, as my reason insisted, he was guilty of no injury to me except an injury so fantastic that only destiny could be blamed, and since, too, he was all unconscious even of that, there must be truce between us.

Yet there rose insistently before me the lissom beauty of his wife. The light that tangled itself in her hair blinded and tortured me.

The deity I had built out of fancy and under the influence of the tropics, laid itself in parallel with the woman I had seen last night. The goddess I knew. The woman I loved and doubted. Was she only the coquette who wanted to lead me chained at her chariot wheel for the cheap joy of conquest? My goddess had not been that sort. What had she to offer me in return for such a tribute to her vanity? Was I merely to flit in the background of her life giving all that the heart has, receiving nothing but the occasional condescension of a smile? Does great beauty so preëmpt a woman's soul as to drive out even the homely virtues?

These questions bored insistently into my brain until it ached with perplexity. Then came the memory of her momentary wistfulness; her craving for something more than life had given her, or something different.

What was that? At all events, I knew that to fall again within the scope of her personality would mean to be swept rudderless from my moorings. Whatever her object, be it exalted or petty, I must inevitably bow to it, in unconditional surrender, if such were her good or evil pleasure. Consequently the one end of all my thinking was the resolve that I should not again see her.

The journey was progressing with more surety than my reflections. It whisked us through the richness of Bluegrass pasture lands, and the opulent ease of Bluegrass life into a barer country where the color of the soil grew mean and outcropping rocks lay bare. The landscape, as though in keeping with my mood, dropped down a scale of bleakness.

The cleanliness of dignified mansions, spacious barns and whitewashed fences gave place to less pretentious farm-houses in disrepair, and these in turn dwindled to log cabins that were hardly better than shanties, and choking undergrowth instead of clean meadows.

We roared through foothills where the vivid green of young cedars dashed the gray tangle of naked timber and scrub. At last we climbed into the mountains themselves, lying in dreary ramparts of isolation under skies that had grown sodden and raw. Here were the barriers of the Cumberland heaping up gigantic piles of raggedness under bristling needle points of timber.

We passed through anomalous villages where the nation's most primitive and quarantined life was rubbing shoulders with the outriders of capital's invasion. Shaggy men ridden in from distant cabins on shaggier horses; men who probably nursed guilty knowledge of illicit stills, gazed at the passing train out of humorless and illiterate eyes.

At last we left the train at a station over which the November dusk was closing, where the coke furnaces glared in red spots along the shadowed ridges. A four-mile drive brought us to the tawdry hotel, and after attacking our eggs and ham we went to our rooms. I on a feather bed, with the reek of a low-turned lamp in my nostrils, lay for hours gazing at the patched and dirty wall-paper, and at last fell asleep to dream of a wonderful lady who opened a door in a wall of rock, and led me through it to things which could never be.

The next morning as we waited for the wagon which was to take us twenty miles into the hills, Weighborne showed me the dingy court-house whose weatherbeaten walls had in other days been penetrated by the gatling guns of the militia. He pointed out boyish-looking figures whose eyes were young and mild, yet who had more than once "notched their guns." He showed me spots where this marked man or that had fallen, shot to death from the court-house windows, by assassins who had never been apprehended or prosecuted.

"That is all changing," he said. "When capital comes the feud must go."

Stolid groups of mountaineers, clad in butternut and jeans, eyed us with mild curiosity. Here and there a father whose face was as stupid and uneducated as that of a Russian peasant, walked side by side with a son dressed in the season's ready-made styles. Between parent and child yawned the gulf of schooling, which the younger generation had acquired in a college "down below" or in the new schools at home, presided over by "fotched on" teachers.

We traveled at snail's pace over twisting roads where our wagon strained and creaked in tortuous ruts almost hub-deep, and where the scraggly horses lay against their collars and tugged valiantly at the traces. Quail started up before us with their whir of softly drumming wings and disappeared into the thick cover of timber. Squirrels barked and scampered to hiding at our coming. Occasionally a fox whisked out of sight with a contemptuous flirt of its brush. Once only in twenty miles we encountered another traveler. An old man, riding bareback on a mule, drew up in the road and awaited us. Despite the cold, a gap of sockless, dust-covered ankle showed between his rough brogan uppers and the wrinkled legs of his butternut breeches. Across his mule's withers balanced a rifle. His face was bearded and sad.

"Mornin' Rat-Ankle," drawled our driver, halting the team for converse.

"Mornin', Pate," came the nasal reply.

There was a long interval of silence while the mounted man contemplated us with an unabashed stare. Finally he spoke again.

"Mornin', strangers," he said.

There followed a protracted series of questionings between the native born as to the health and well being of their respective families.

I thought I saw the mountaineer's eyes glitter with sudden interest when Weighborne's name was given him, but the light died quickly out of his pupils, leaving only the weariness and sadness of his dull life.

At times the climbs were so steep that we had to trudge alongside, lending a hand at the wheels. The last two miles of the journey, said our driver, would be impassable for a wheeled vehicle. He would have to deposit us and our luggage at Chicken-Gizzard Creek. A little later, while we were walking up a steep incline, Weighborne drew me back out of earshot of the teamster.

"I'd better post you on a few details," he said. "Ever hear of the Keithley assassination?"

I shook my head.

"Keithley was the prosecuting attorney in some rather celebrated murder trials. He was shot to death one afternoon as he came out of the court-room."

"Yes?" I questioned.

"Six months later Con Hoover was shot from the laurel on this road. He had allied himself with those who sought to avenge Keithley."

I nodded my head.

"There were Cale Springer, Bud Dode—I could enumerate other victims, but that is all unnecessary detail. What concerns us is this. Jim Garvin is county judge. In a rough way he is the political boss of the region and he has built up a fortune. His own gun is unnotched, but a half-dozen men who have incurred his displeasure have come to abrupt ends. The newspapers in Louisville and Lexington have intimated that besides being at the head of fiscal affairs and operating a general store the judge also issues his orders to a murder syndicate."

"Why," I demanded in some disgust, "hasn't it been proven?"

"It is difficult to prove things of this sort—when the defendant is more powerful than the law and when juries walk in terror," Weighborne reminded me. "He has twice been tried for complicity. A company of state guards patrolled the court-house yard to reassure venire-men and witnesses. The only result was the defeat, at the next election, of the judge and prosecutor who had made themselves obnoxious."

"Why," I inquired, "aren't such malefactors taken into a civilized circuit, on a change of venue, and tried where jurors are not intimidated?"

"They have been—with the same result," affirmed my informant. "You see, while the jurors were freed from fear, the witnesses knew they must return home."

"Shall we be likely to meet this highly interesting character?" I questioned.

"The store where our wagon turns back," said Weighborne, "is his place."

"Then I am to be careful not to form or express any opinion adverse to judicious homicide? Is that the point?"

Weighborne smiled.

"Our plans involve bringing a branch railroad along the way we have been traveling," he replied, "and the coming of that railroad means the death knell of Jim Garvin's power. What is still more to the point, our attorney here and the man for whose house we are bound is the Hon. Calloway Marcus. He was Keithley's law partner, and he is a marked man. He it was who prosecuted Garvin—and lost his official head. His actual head he keeps on his shoulders by riding at the center of a bodyguard. I tell you these matters so that you may watch your words."

"Shall we encounter open hostility at this place?" I inquired.

Weighborne shook his head. "On the contrary, we shall be most courteously received. Politeness is highly esteemed hereabouts. The fact that a man means to 'lay-way' you to-night, with a squirrel gun, is not deemed sufficient reason for relaxing his courtesy this afternoon."

An hour later our conveyance drew up at the junction of two ragged roads where thin, outcropping ledges of limestone went down to the rim of a shallow stream. Beyond the water rose a beetling bluff. One could imagine that when summer brought to this hollow in the hills its richness of green, and its profusion of trumpet flower and laurel and rhododendron, there must be an eye-filling beauty, but now it was unspeakably raw and desolate.

Two houses were in sight and both were of depressing ugliness. In the fork of the road where the ground was trodden hard stood the "store." It was a one-room shack built of logs and boarded over, but innocent of paint. A leanto porch, disfigured by a few advertising signs, gave entrance to a narrow door. The second house set back and higher up the slope of the mountain. Its solidity was that of mortised logs and its windows were protected behind solid shutters. Inside there was plainly an abundance of space, as befitted the dwelling-place of the district's overlord. A clump of white-armed sycamores partly masked its front, but through the naked branches one could see that for a hundred yards about it, in every direction, lay unbroken clearing, and that for all its civilian seeming it might, if need arose, stand siege against anything less formidable than gatling guns.

Stamping the cold and cramp from our feet, we settled our score with the liveryman, and turned into the store.

---

# CHAPTER XVIII

## A CHAT WITH A DICTATOR.

Inside Judge Garvin's store we came upon a group of slovenly loungers. Had my mind been free enough of its own troubling thoughts to spare a remnant of interest, I should have found this new and strange scheme of things engrossing. I was in a scrap of America which the onrushing tide of world advancement had left stranded and forgotten. Here a people of unmixed British stock lived primitive lives, fought feudal wars, and shrined every virtue high except regard for human life.

These four narrow walls in part epitomised that life. The shelves back of the counters displayed what things they held essentials: rough crockery, coarse calicoes, canned goods, barrels of brown sugar, brogans, stick candy and ammunition.

About a small stove loafed some eight or ten men and several "hound-dogs." The shoulders of these men slouched; their hands were chapped and coarse; their clothes muddied, but when they walked it was with something of the catamount's softness, and their eyes were alert.

Behind the counter stood a man of fifty. I knew, without waiting for Weighborne's greeting, that this must be Garvin. There was something pronounced yet hard to define which gave him the outstanding prominence of a master among minions.

He was a large man and inclined to stoutness. His hair and moustache were sandy and his florid face was marked with a purplish tracery of veins in which the blood appeared to bank and stand currentless. His neck was grossly heavy and bovine, but his forehead was broad and his eyes disarmingly frank and blue. His mouth, too, fell into the kindly lines of a perpetual smile.

His clothing was rough and his neck collarless, but one forgot this and noted only the suavity of his bearing and the ingratiating quality of his voice. Such was the man who should have gone long ago to death or imprisonment for the orders he had issued to his assassins.

"Judge Garvin," said my companion, "my name's Weighborne. I met you once in the court-house. You probably don't remember me."

The gigantic reprobate smiled affably.

"Sure, I remember you," he affirmed. "I mighty seldom forget a man." He came out from his place of office behind the counter and proffered his hand. It was not, like those of his henchmen, a calloused hand.

I had leisure to glance about the faces of the group as this colloquy occurred. They had been stolidly silent, gazing at us with unconcealed curiosity. When Weighborne introduced himself there was no overt display of interest, and yet unless I was allowing my imagination to run away with me I sensed from that moment forward that the lazy indolence of the atmosphere was electrified. The men lounged about in unchanged attitudes and from time to time spat on the hot stove, yet each of them was carefully appraising us.

"I reckon you gentlemen came up to look over this here coal and timber project?" Garvin's voice seemed to hold only a politely simulated interest in our affairs.

Weighborne nodded.

"Do you think, Judge, as a man in good position to gauge the sentiment of the people, that we shall have their sympathy in our efforts?"

I studied Garvin's face closely, but if there was a spark of interest in his eyes, my eyes could not detect it. He smiled noncommittally and shook his head.

"Well, now, as to that," he replied judicially, "I couldn't hardly say."

"We want to develop the coal and timber interests of the section," summarized Weighborne briefly. "It will mean railroad facilities, better schools and fuller enforcement of the law."

Garvin nodded in a fashion of reserved approval. There was no betrayed hint of his perfect understanding that it meant other things as well: an end of "Garvinism," a period to his baronial powers; the imminent danger which lurked for him in courts no longer afraid to try, and witnesses no longer terrified into perjury.

"That sounds purty promisin'," he agreed. "It sounds purty good."

"Then why would the people not coöperate?"

Garvin gave the question deliberate consideration.

"Well, now," he finally said, "that ain't such an easy question to answer just right off. The people hereabouts have been livin' purty much the same way fer nigh onto a hundred years. They're satisfied."

"Are they satisfied with a reign of terror?" Weighborne was treading the thin ice of local conditions. I fancied he was trying to force Garvin into committing himself, but it was a dangerous experiment.

"What's anybody terrified about?" inquired the Judge with entire blindness.

Weighborne, totally checkmated by this childlike query, changed ground and laughed.

"Oh, we hear a good deal of talk down below," he explained, "about the shot from the laurel and all that sort of thing."

Judge Garvin laughed heartily.

"Oh, pshaw!" he exclaimed in high good-humor. "There ain't nothin' in all that. Them newspapers down below's jest obliged to have somethin' to talk about. We're all neighbors up here. We're simple sort of folks. Sometimes we has our little arguments, but—" the lips still smiled genially; he paused and his voice was like a benediction as he went on—"but I hope we ain't got in no such serious fix that we needs regulatin' from outside. They do say that most of them fellers that got killed needed killin' pretty bad. I've lost two brothers, but I ain't kickin'."

Weighborne saw that a withdrawal from debate would be advisable, but that this withdrawal must not seem precipitate.

"However, as a matter of argument," he suggested, "is any man competent to decide that his enemy needs killing?"

The judge went into his trousers-pocket and produced a twist of tobacco into which he bit generously before replying.

"Well," he drawled, "your enemy's the man that's goin' to decide whether you need killin'. Why don't it work both ways?"

Weighborne made no reply. One cannot argue with a set opinion. The loungers were saying nothing, but their eyes dwelt admiringly on their spokesman. At last Garvin smilingly inquired:

"You'd have to condemn rights-of-way, I reckon?"

"Only where we couldn't make individual trades," answered my companion.

"That procedure ain't apt to be no ways popular," reflected Judge Garvin.

"You gentlemen understand I ain't criticisin'," he assured us when we made no reply. "If condemnation suits are brought in my co'te I ain't got no personal interests to serve. I'm jest namin' it to you, because you asked about the people's notions, that's all."

"At least," fenced Weighborne, "you yourself see the advantages of development?"

It was putting a question which was almost a challenge to this leader of the old, lawless order whose baronial power we threatened. He answered it with no flicker of visible interest in his pleasant drawl.

"Well, as to that, what little property I've got would be benefited, but as an officer of the law, I reckon it wouldn't hardly be proper for me to take no sides." A moment later he hospitably added, "If there's any courtesy I can show you gentlemen just call on me. Where are you goin' to stop at?"

I gazed on this lord of lies with compelled fascination. Under a crude exterior and a suavity which gave the impression of stupid good-nature he was masking bitter and intense feeling. Here was a tyrant talking with men who represented the new order and he knew as well as we that if we succeeded his carefully built scheme must topple. Our success and his could not both have life. One must perish. The power that had enriched him, a power built on murder and stealth, must go from him, leaving him only the contempt of his fellows—or he must thwart our designs. One might have expected such dissimulation in a polished diplomat moving the strategic pieces of the chessboard of some European power, but here it seemed inconceivable.

"We are on our way over to the Calloway Marcus place," explained my companion in a casual voice.

There was no change of expression on the face of the storekeeper, though the name was one he venomously hated. One or two of the more unguarded loungers scowled in silence.

"How did you calc'late to git thar?" asked Garvin. "It's all of two miles an' they're rough miles—mostly straight up an' down."

"I suppose we shall have to walk," said Weighborne.

"I'd like to take you over thar," said the judge thoughtfully, "I sure would, but the fact is me and Cal Marcus ain't got much in common an'—well, you understand how it is?"

We thanked him for his solicitude and at the same moment one of the henchmen drew him aside and spoke in a low voice. Garvin came back and addressed us again.

"Curt Dawson says Cal Marcus went past here this mornin', goin' to'rds town. It's an hour by sun now—he'd ought to be comin' back this way before long."

I have spoken at length of Garvin and have given only collective notice to the group of mountaineers who loafed about the dingy store, because aside from their more savage qualities they were much like the indolent loungers one may see in any cross-roads grocery. Even viewed as feudists, and I was so new to the country that I was inclined to discount the somber and murderous stories of their ways, they were still merely the members of a human wolf pack and much alike. Only this shrewd leader stood out in personal relief.

But to this generalizing there must be one exception, and that was to be found in the person of Curt Dawson. Until he came forward and drew his chief aside, I had not noticed him and he had not emerged from his seat in a darkened corner while we had chatted. When he did come forth it was with a step at once indolent and suggestive of power. His movements were all unhurried, even graceful, but every flexing and tensing of his muscles carried a hint of potential swiftness and power. His face was unshaven and dissolute, but it retained a keen and instinctive intelligence. His gray eyes had a light in them that seemed to come from some inner source.

Curt Dawson could hardly have been more than thirty and was in the full prime of his youthful strength, hard as hickory and in the same rough fashion as the pines among which he had grown, commanding in appearance and pungent in personality. I found my eyes dwelling on him, and later on this scrutiny bore results. No one who had once seen this young desperado could fail to recognize him on second meeting. His manner of addressing the judge carried the assurance of the confidential man, and a certain arrogance of demeanor.

We had left our bags outside and I took up a position near the door where I could watch the twisting ruts of the drab road. We talked, as we waited, of the outside world and Garvin astonished me by his grasp on general affairs.

At last Marcus arrived and his coming made a strange picture which dwells still in my mind. The western sky was all ash of rose and the higher clouds were dark masses edged with gold. The hills were gray and frowning ramparts with bristling crests. Against this setting, around the shoulder of the mountain, appeared a grotesque cortège.

A half-score of rough men mounted on unkempt horses came slowly and gloomily into view. They maintained, as they rode, the slovenly formation of a hollow square and across their pommels lay repeating rifles. The battered rims of their felt hats drooped over sharp-featured faces.

The only unarmed member of the group rode at the center of the square. He was tall and unspeakably gaunt. One looked at his worn and rugged face and thought of the earlier portraits of Abraham Lincoln; the portraits of lean and battling days. The collar of his threadbare overcoat was upturned, but at the opening one had the glimpse of a narrow black necktie slipped askew. The clean-shaven line of his mouth was set in relentless determination.

The bodyguard rode with hanging reins, and each right hand lay in counterfeited carelessness on the lock of its rifle.

"Thar he comes now," commented Garvin. "You must excuse me if I don't go out to introduce you. He's a bitter kind of feller. You understand how it is."

At Weighborne's signal his attorney halted and the men of the bodyguard drew rein, keeping their places about him. We walked out to the middle of the road, and while we talked to the rawboned, life-battered man in the center of the hollow square, his attendants shouted greetings to the loungers on the porch of the store. These greetings partook of the nature of pleasantries and the only note of frank hostility came from the throats of the hounds. They bristled and growled with an instinct which was softened by no artificial code of hypocrisy. Still, so long as the halt lasted, the two parties kept their eyes alertly fixed on each other. It needed little penetration to discover that the geniality was shallow and temporary, like that between the outposts of hostile armies lying close-camped, across an interval soon to be closed in battle.

"You made a very unfortunate mistake in stopping here," said Marcus to Weighborne, in a low voice. He nodded to two mountaineers who rode on the far side of the cavalcade. They slipped from their saddles and allowed us to mount in their stead while they trudged alongside, carrying our bags.

As we started forward, Weighborne answered.

"I didn't halt at Garvin's place from choice. The wagon could go no further. I don't suppose there was any actual danger, and after all I wanted to see how he would talk."

Marcus nodded and drew his mouth tighter.

"It turns out all right," he said, "but don't do it again."

After a moment's silence he burst out bitterly.

"No danger! My God, man, do you suppose I ride like this—surrounded by armed men, because it pleases my pride?" He swept his talon-like hand around him in a circle. "Look at them! Do you reckon I do that for pomp and display? Do you suppose any man likes to say good-bye to his children when he leaves home with the thought in his mind that it may be a last good-bye?"

"Is it as bad as that?" I questioned with the stranger's incredulity.

He turned his hunted eyes on me. "Worse," he said briefly. "I dare not go unguarded from my house to my barn, sir. Keithley used to carry his two-year-old child into court in his arms. Even they would not shoot a baby. One day he went without the child. That day he died."

I looked at the face which was turned toward me. It was a face from which had been whipped the knowledge of how to smile. We rode for a half-mile in silence with only the cuppy thud of hoofs on the soft earth, the creaking of stirrup leather and the clink of bit rings.

"Why," I asked at last, "don't you leave such a country and establish yourself where you can have security?"

His angular chin came up with a jerk. His eyes flashed.

"Go away?" he repeated. "Do you think a man wants to be driven from the country where he and his parents and his children were born? Besides, sir, my mother belongs to the old order. I was the first to be educated. She still smokes her pipe in the chimney-corner. She is of the mountains. She must stay here." He paused, then his words began again dispassionately, and gathered, as he talked, the fiery resonance of the instinctive orator.

"If the men who love war, leave lawless countries, who in God's name is to do the work? The order is changing. What does Kipling say about the men who blaze trails?

"'On the sand-drift, on the veldt-side, in the fern-scrub we lay,That our sons might follow after by the bones on the way.'

"These men have made a mockery of the law. It is my desire to punish them with the law. It is my purpose to do so unless they kill me first. Why am I representing your company? For the fee? No, sir!... God knows I need the fee, but I shall also have a bigger compensation. When the new order comes I shall see Garvin's power crumple. I shall send him to the gallows or to the penitentiary. That will be my reward." His voice was again passionate. "The filthy assassin realizes my motive and he sees in you my allies. Watch him, and safeguard your steps."

---

# CHAPTER XIX

## A VOLLEY FROM THE LAUREL.

When we reached the attorney's house the reality of feud conditions gained corroboration from a hundred small details. Like Garvin's, it stood in an area stripped of trees and undergrowth. It was a large cabin of logs and to its original two rooms rambling additions had from time to time been made. Everywhere a note of the poor and primitive stood out in uncouth nakedness. The men of the guard were all impoverished kinsmen, who lived like parasites upon the lawyer's strained and meager bounty. Several of them slept on pallets in a loft gained by a ladder, and others dwelt in near-by cabins. The room turned over to us served as guest chamber and parlor, and here alone in the house was there any hint of concession to appearances. Through the cracks of its uncarpeted floor chilly gusts of wind swept upward, and sent us hovering quail-like as close as possible to the stone hearth of the broad chimney place. A huge four-post bed in one corner was decorated with stiff pillows upon which purple paper showed through coverings of coarse lace; patches of newspaper stopped the widest wall cracks. A cheap cottage organ stood at one side and rush-bottomed chairs completed the furnishings. A small cuddy-hole housed the attorney and his wife. His mother, an ancient crone-like woman of withered, leathery face, and all her brood of grandchildren slept in two beds in the large, murky room which also accommodated dining table, cook stove and pantry accessories.

One saw a profusion of firearms, and unlike the make-shift of less important things these were modern and effective. Before lamp-lighting came the barring of heavy shutters, and as time passed we grew accustomed to other evidences of that caution which was daily routine with these people living in a practical state of siege. We were fed, in relays, by the flickering light of a coal-oil lamp. The women declined to partake of food until we were through, and busied themselves incessantly between stove and table. As we withdrew to the draughty room which was ours for sleeping, but common ground until bedtime, the retainers shuffled into the places about the table which we had just vacated, for supper, eating, as suited henchmen, after their betters.

We were not a merry party as we huddled in a semi-circle around the hearth where the blaze burned our faces while the gusty air chilled our backs. Weighborne and Marcus argued over an opened copy of Kentucky Reports.

The old woman, with a face shriveled like that of an aged monkey, crouched in her chair and sucked with toothless gums at a clay pipe.

When an hour had thawed the shyness of the mountain folk into general conversation and I had been forced to tell many traveler's tales, Marcus arose and with a rough tenderness wrapped a shawl around the shivering shoulders of the old woman.

"My mother," he said with no note of apology, "has never been to Louisville or traveled on a railroad train. She is afraid of accidents." He turned and shouted into her deaf ear, "Mother, Mr. Deprayne here has crossed the ocean. He's been to the Holy Land."

The old woman lifted her wrinkled eyes and gazed at me, in wonderment.

"Well, Prov-i-*dence*!" she exclaimed. It was her single contribution to the evening's conversation.

Once a dog barked, and with silent promptness two or three of the younger men melted out into the night to reconnoiter.

The visitor proved to be only a neighbor seeking to borrow some farm implement and he announced himself from afar with proper assurance that he came as a friend. We heard his voice drawing nearer and shouting: "It's me. I'm a-comin' in."

I was for the most part a listener, offering few contributions to the talk. I was thinking of other matters, but before the evening came to an end I had heard, in plain unvarnished recital, stories which began to make the spirit of the vendetta comprehensible. I spoke of Curt Dawson and asked our host for a biography. The mountain lawyer's rugged face grew dark with feeling.

"I have twice prosecuted him," he said bitterly. "And in the chain of evidence I wove around him there was no weak link, but a conviction would have been a personal defiance of Garvin. That required courage. Each time the foreman of the panel came in with perjury on his lips and reported 'not guilty.'" He paused and then went on. "When Keithley fell in the court-house yard, and while the rifle smoke was still curling from a jury-room window, I rushed into the place and I found this boy there. He was wiping gun grease from his hands, and he testified that he had heard the shot while passing and had come in to detect the assassin. Of course, he was the murderer. He has other crimes of the same type to his damnable discredit. He is Garvin's principal gun-fighter. Garvin has never fired a shot in accomplishment of his crimes. His men have all been slain by proxy. Curt Dawson has become so notorious that of late Garvin has kept him as much as possible out of sight. I am a little surprised that he mentioned Dawson's name to you. He has of late rather pursued the policy of holding ostensibly aloof, and he might have inferred that you would repeat the circumstances to me." Marcus rose and paced the cabin floor for a few turns, then came back and took his seat once more in the circle about the fire.

"You mean," suggested Weighborne, "that the implication of Dawson was coming too close to identifying the master hand?"

The lawyer nodded. "It is well understood that Dawson is merely a part of Garvin. That makes it unwise to give him great prominence. If he has been called back it means something."

"And you think that something is—?" Weighborne left the question unfinished.

"I think that when the buzzards come there is apt to be carrion." The thin, close lips of the attorney closed tightly.

"I have always understood that this man is to be my executioner some day. Maybe the time is closer at hand than I anticipated."

"Is this fellow totally illiterate or has he, like Garvin, a shrewd knowledge of things?" I inquired.

"He has had only scant and primary schooling, but he has learned a great deal that is not in books. He has seen the outer world as a railroad brakeman and when still a boy went to the Klondike.... Let me impress this on you both. At any time you see him don't fail to tell me at once the full particulars ... I had supposed him to be in Virginia. If he's here now he will bear some watching."

The two hours between early supper and early bedtime dragged along tediously. The old woman sat dozing and nodding while two of the retainers sang to the accompaniment of the cottage organ, strange songs, half-folk lore, in weird, nasal voices that rose high and shrill. This singing was without musical effect, for the mountaineer alters his voice in song and unconsciously adopts the tradition of the Chinese stage, achieving a thin falsetto. It was a relief when the men climbed their ladder and our host bade us good-night.

Early morning found me awake, but already someone had hospitably kindled our fire, and when we went out on to the porch, where a tin basin and gourd dipper supplied the only bathing facilities, a small tow-headed boy was there before us with hot, water in a saucepan. The mountaineer is averse to cold water and sparing with hot. It was presumed that we shared this prejudice.

Frost still hung thick on the stubble and the mists lingered in the valleys when we climbed into our saddles and trailed out to inspect one of the tracts in which we were interested.

I was not a happy man nor one bearing a blithe spirit, for my own discoveries crowded too closely and heavily on my heart, to be lightened by the mere novelty of fresh surroundings. Yet even in my shadowed state of mind, I could not help drinking in the splendidly unpolluted air with deep breaths that made my lungs feel new. From frost-rimmed earth to infinity it seemed to stretch in clean and filtered clarity. The mountains were no longer ragged piles of chocolate and slate. The fresh vigor of morning had folded them in the softening dyes of a dozen inspiriting colors. Distance merged the leafless trees into veil-like masses of dove browns and grays where shadows of violet lurked and deepened. The woods wore a brave, if ragged, coat of russet and burgundy and orange with a strong hint of that purple which is the proper garb of kings and hills. As we rode along ridges we looked down into vast basins of variegated country, rough but essentially beautiful. On the lips of the young day was a silent bugle-call of color. Above and about us the high-piled barriers of the mountains clambered steeply into space where the sky was blue and tuneful.

I understood why Marcus had so resentfully repudiated the suggestion of turning his back on this country. I knew that a man whose eyes had first opened on such scenes would not wish that their last gaze should be exiled. Rough and hard as life among these peaks might be, there brooded a spirit here which would make flight impossible. The roots of the laurel would hold the native son planted where his life had come to bud and leaf. The eagle's brood would not go down to seek the easy security of prim orchards and smooth meadows.

We rode sometimes for hours on end without seeing a cabin. Then we would come upon a rude habitation of logs and pause to pass greetings with a gaunt man in butternut brown, and would catch a glimpse of tow-headed children and slatternly women.

So civil were all these salutations; so at variance with any idea of violence that the elaborate precautions of Marcus (the very fashion in which we were now riding armed and *en cortège*) began to assume a ludicrous grotesquerie.

Of course, I argued with myself, the attorney knew his own country and I did not, yet I was morally certain that Weighborne and I could have gone about our business unescorted and as secure as though we were inspecting suburban lots under the guidance of a real-estate dealer. I suggested something of the sort to Marcus and his only response for the moment was a grim smile. Then he patiently began to explain.

"At this moment," he said, "Jim Garvin knows just where we are and just what we're doing. We have spoken to three men. Of that three at least two have notified the store of our passing. There is a 'phone at Chicken Gizzard, you know."

It seemed rather too exaggerated a system of espionage for probability.

"And telephoning in this country," went on the attorney, "is not so simple a matter as you might suppose. We have no general system and no universal exchange. There are telephones or 'boxes' as they are locally called, connecting three or four houses into separate groups. A telephone message from my house to Lexington, for example, would have to be repeated and relayed through a half-dozen 'boxes' before it reached its destination."

And yet during all that day's ride and all of the next three days there was never, to my eye, an indication that any man interested himself in our goings or comings. On the fourth day it was otherwise.

We had covered some twenty-five or thirty miles since breakfast over roads that were full of climbs and other places where there were no roads at all. Our spent horses plodded wearily, though the sun hung close enough over the western highlands to warn us that, unless we increased our pace, we should be benighted.

We were riding with our ever-present squad of gunmen and our road dipped to the valley where we should cross that branch of Chicken Gizzard which bounded the Marcus place at the back. We shook our jaded mounts into a shambling trot and reached it at that hour which ushers in the short November dusk. The woods were still and the bark of a belated squirrel going home from forage broke the silence with a seeming of noisiness.

The creek was shallow and fordable, but to reach the crossing it was necessary to follow a dizzy bridle path steeply downward and in single file, between thick growing saplings and laurel. Back of the mountains the sky held a pale afterglow against which the higher timber sketched itself starkly. The body of the woods was a dark mass out of which only the white-barked sycamores showed themselves with any clearness of individuality.

Beyond the ribbon of water lay Marcus's rotting and weed-choked division fence. The smoke from his chimney, and the glint at the crack of a lighted window were visible a half-mile distant.

Our front horses had splashed fetlock deep into the water and halted the cavalcade to drink when a sudden staccato outbreak ripped the silence. Three thin jets of rifle fire blinked out with acrid sharpness from the laurel through which we had just come. The men who had ambushed us must have lain so close to our passing line that we might almost have touched them from our saddles as we rode down the declivity.

There was instantly a confused, snorting, splashing stampede for the cover of the opposite shore. I, who chanced to be riding third in line, followed my two leaders and made the timber in safety. I slid from my saddle and found refuge in a tangle of drift at the roots of a sycamore which overhung the water. My armament was limited to an automatic pistol, small enough for the pocket, and it hardly warranted intrusion into a debate with repeating rifles. As chance would have it, just as our cavalcade had halted, and the instant before the volley was fired, I had half-turned in my saddle to gaze back, at the two-color effect of the slate-gray hills and lemon sky. Every other face was looking forward, and I alone saw a figure standing above, in the brief illumination of a rifle flash. It was the figure of Curt Dawson. Those of our party who found themselves in the rear and hampered, in their escape, by the confusion ahead, dismounted in the stream and began maneuvering to the opposite shore at an angle which gave them protection behind the bodies of their mounts. As they came they fired with random aim at the points from which had spurted the ambuscading fire. But over the hill had settled a sudden and profound quiet. The darkness had spoiled markmanship which was presumably selected for its efficiency.

It appeared that every one had made the crossing unharmed, though for a few minutes each man held to such concealment as he had attained and there was no effort to reunite.

At last, like disorganized partridges coming back to the covey, we crawled out of our individual hiding-places and began collecting on the trail-like path which went twisting up to the house. Some led their horses and some, who like myself had been separated from their beasts, came on foot.

As we gathered without a sound the mountaineers were searching the timber with wide eyes that contended against the darkness.

Then came the startling outburst of a fresh volley. It was fired into the group and fired from cover on the attorney's own property. I felt a sensation not unlike a hornet sting in my left shoulder and clapped my right hand against the spot. I did not fall. I even had a sense of surprise at the comparative mildness and painlessness of the pang. I heard some one fall heavily, but in the darkness it was impossible to distinguish individuals. So close on the assassin's shots that they were hardly distinguishable came the cracks of our own guns, and without giving the concealed riflemen time to shift positions our men charged into the ambush.

Our policy was no longer one of retreat, but of attack. I saw a tall youth plough his way through the thicket toward a clump of cedar which had just belched fire, and having to do something, I followed at his heels. The silence had given way now to the ripping of bushes and the kicking up of dead leaves, and twice off at my side I heard the pop-popping of rifles. I, following my guide, was crouching and slipping from tree trunk to laurel bush and from laurel bush to boulder. Suddenly a spurt of flame and a report burst out in our faces, and the song of a bullet passing near made me duck my head. Then the man with me fired and there was a groan from the front and the crash of a body falling into a bush.

Afterward (I suppose in a very few minutes) quiet settled again, except for the treading of our men as they searched the timber. The assailants were clearly driven off. My companion even ventured to bend down as we returned and strike a match over the fallen body in the brush. As it flared up, I recognized with a shock, the thin, saddened face of the sockless man who had accosted us in the road, and whom our driver had called Rat-Ankle. He now lay doubled in a shapeless heap, and dead.

We already knew that the casualties had not been one-sided, and as my companion and I regained the road among the first we saw that some one still lay there, his horse standing quietly over him. A glance told me that it was Weighborne. His bulky size even in that crumpled attitude unmistakably proclaimed him. As we bent over him, we found that he was unconscious but breathing, and we hoisted him up to an empty saddle, where we held him as we made the trip to the house.

# CHAPTER XX

## A CAVALCADE FROM THE LAUREL.

I have since searchingly asked myself whether, at that time, any mean thought entered my mind as to the possibilities which might open for me if Weighborne died. I set it down in justification, though it may rather be attributable to the excitement of the moment than to inherent guilelessness, that that phase of the matter did not occur to me. Had I entertained such speculations they must have been short lived, for when we arrived at the cabin and made an examination, and when later by relayed telephone messages we brought the doctor, it was to learn that the patient would have to lie in bed for perhaps a week or two, but need fear no grave consequences. His wound had narrowly missed the heart, but the margin was sufficient. My own injury proved to be a mere flesh scratch and a bandage did for it all that was needful.

I was rather surprised at the almost lethargic calmness with which the household greeted our disordered homecoming. Preparations for supper went on with little interruption. There was no excited demand from those who had stayed at home, for the full story, and even the children seemed uninquisitive. Only the aged woman showed a flash of unexpected fire as she demanded, "Didn't ye git nary one of *them*?"

"We got Rat-Ankle," drawled an unshaven lout with a revolting note of placid satisfaction.

"That's better'n not gettin' nary one," commended the old woman. Her voice revealed the hereditary source of Marcus' ability for sincere hating.

I looked at her aged, monkey-like face and the intensity of her beady eyes with wonderment. There was vindictiveness there but no fear, no excitement even, except the excitement of hate—and yet this old woman was the same who could not be induced to travel on a railroad train for fear of an accident.

It was several hours later that the doctor arrived. He was much like the men among whom he lived. If he had once been otherwise long association had roughened him to their own similitude. He entered with a wordless nod and went straight to the bed where the injured man lay unconscious. After a silent examination he opened his worn and faded saddle-bags and proceeded taciturnly but capably with his work. He asked no questions and Marcus volunteered no explanation. At last he rose and said, "He ain't in no

- 118 -

great danger if he keeps quiet. Have you got a little licker in the house, Calloway?"

Before the fireplace he poured generously from a stoneware jug into a tin cup, but instead of tossing down his white whiskey at a gulp he sipped it slowly, while he gave directions to the lawyer or shouted them loudly into the ear of the old woman. The only allusion to the ambuscade came from her.

"Our folks got Rat-Ankle," she announced somewhat triumphantly. "But they didn't see nary other face of them that lay-wayed 'em."

"Don't pay no attention to Mother," said Marcus more hastily than I had before heard him speak; "at times she gets childish."

The physician nodded.

Then it was that I, in an ignorance which had not learned the valuable art of general distrust, volunteered a remark for which my host, so soon as we were alone, rebuked me sternly.

"Mrs. Marcus is mistaken as to that," I said. "Just as the volley was fired, I recognized Curt Dawson."

The voice of Calloway Marcus again cut in with an interruption. "Oh, I reckon you're mistaken about that, Mr. Deprayne. I understand Dawson is across the Virginia line."

"I'm sure enough," I persisted, failing entirely to catch my host's effort to silence me, "to swear to it in court."

"Mr. Deprayne is a stranger here," deprecated the lawyer. "He isn't familiar enough with our people to be certain in these matters."

Again the doctor nodded and, taking up his saddle-bags, went out. As soon as he had bidden him farewell, Marcus returned. He walked over and stood before me with a face that was deeply troubled. Except for his mother, too deaf to hear his low-pitched voice, and Weighborne, whose initial unconsciousness had passed under medical administrations into a profound sleep, we were alone.

"Sir," he said patiently, "I can't be angry with you because you don't understand what you have done. Perhaps I should have warned you. I sent for Richardson because he was the only doctor within many hours' riding, but I don't confide in him. He will carry straight to Garvin your announcement that you have recognized his gun-man. You have given away a secret I might have used to great advantage. Sir, you have tremendously complicated matters."

He dropped his hands at his sides with a weary gesture, half-despair. "However, it's done now," he added, "it's no use to deplore it—but, for God's sake, be more careful in the future."

When Weighborne recovered consciousness he spoke to me once more of his wife. He was afraid that an exaggerated report of the affair would leak through to the Lexington papers, and he wished to allay her anxiety. The duty of this reassurance devolved on me, but the complicated system of telephoning spared me the torture of felicitating her. The message was relayed through disinterested voices before it reached her ears. As it eventuated Weighborne's precaution was a wise one since the news filtered that same night to a newspaper correspondent at the railroad town. This scribe so well utilized his information that the papers of the next morning carried scare-heads over a story of bloodshed and massacre which accorded to both of us desperate wounds and ludicrously lauded us as heroes.

It cannot be said for Weighborne that he proved a docile patient. He had all the energetic man's aversion to inactive days in bed, and he greatly preferred, if he must submit to such an exigency, that it be in his own bed and among more plentiful conveniences, than could be afforded here. But to move him over twenty semi-perpendicular miles was pronounced impossible and to that decree he had to submit.

I, who, despite my newspaper peril, was not even bedridden, continued the daily rides to tracts marked for inspection, and discussed the day's work with him in the evening.

One afternoon we met in the road a party of horsemen who halted us and expressed the desire for a peaceable parley. Marcus gave his assurance and a stout fellow with a ruddy, good-natured face and a benevolent smile rode out and accosted us.

"You're a lawyer, Calloway," he began, "an' I reckon you know I've got to do my duty. I hope you ain't holdin' hit ergainst me none." He paused and seemed relieved when the attorney nodded his understanding.

"I just want ter know ef you won't bring yer fellers ter county co'te any day this week that suits you an' answer fer the killin' of Rat-Ankle. I'm namin' it to yer like a friend, an' I'm askin' you ter set the day. Hit ain't nothin' but a matter of givin' bail noways."

"For whom have you warrants?" asked Marcus.

The sheriff read a list of a half-dozen names, all kinsmen and retainers of the attorney. Weighborne and myself were not included. Marcus accepted service and agreed to be present on the date named. It was not until the sheriff's men had waved their hands and ridden away that he turned to me.

"That shows Garvin's effrontery," he remarked with a laugh. "He summonses me to answer in his own court, for meeting with hostility the attack of his own assassins. I'll be there—but I hope to give him a surprise."

Weighborne had some temperature and was often restless on his mattress of corn shucks, though his amiability held steady. One evening several days after our ambuscade, I was sitting alone and morose before the open hearth while he slept. Since our apartment had been a sickroom, the evening gatherings had been suspended and I had companionship only from my pipe and thoughts. The thoughts were not cheery comrades to-night. They went back with a brutal sort of insistence to the island and the things which had there taken root, to grow with the rank and lawless swiftness of the tropics. I had had a long conversation with Marcus that evening in which he had outlined his plans for the examining trials. He meant to strike a bold and unexpected blow, using me as his star witness.

All that the county judge could do would be to fix a bond for answering to the grand jury, but the circuit court was also under the influence of the dictator, and later when the trials came up on that docket the prosecution would become persecution. Garvin would, however, fix a light bond, he thought, in the preliminary hearing and would expect Marcus to await the main issue later. Therefore, he meant to forestall the attack with an attack in the county court. His enemies would rely on his reputation as a supporter of law and order to make his warfare a warfare within the law, and that would also lull them into expecting only formal and preparatory fencing at the hearing of next Wednesday.

"When I take the course which I mean to take," the attorney had assured me, "it will be in the nature of exploding a bomb and may precipitate trouble. If I had the power to do so I should ask for a militia detachment to be present and preserve order, but unfortunately such a call can come only from some civil officer such as the circuit judge—and he is not disposed to act on my request. I shall have to satisfy myself with having in town every anti-Garvin man whom I can bring there. Garvin doesn't want a general battle just now. He doesn't want to attract outside clamor. He wants to move in the dark, so I think he will instruct against an outbreak in the streets or court-room. But there is one thing I can do, and that I am arranging. I am held in some respect by the papers of Louisville and Lexington, and I have written a rather full statement of conditions here and asked that reporters be present in the court-room on Wednesday. That will mean that whatever transpires cannot be hushed up. Then I shall move to swear Garvin off the bench, announcing openly that his jackal led this ambuscade in obedience to his own orders. That will be my surprise and my proof of it will be your testimony. If he suspected it he would find a way to silence you. Even as it is he knows you recognized Dawson and you must be cautious. He may seek to keep you out of court."

At length I slipped out and stood for a while leaning against a post of the porch, although the air was sharp with frost, and the stars pierced coldly through the hard steel of a winter sky. My other skies had been softer.

The mountains, under a young moon, stood out black and forbidding; frost mists hung like frozen smoke on the lowlands. From somewhere about the house came the nasal singing of a mountaineer to the plunking of a tuneless banjo. His voice rose and quavered and fell with more care that his words be distinct than that his notes be true. He had chosen a song composed by a local bard, and as I stood gazing off across the sea of moonlight and mist he alone broke and tortured the silence.

"Right down here in Adamson coun-teeWhere they have no church of our Lord,Frank Smith sold Pate Art'b'ry some whis-keyAnd caused him to get shot in the for'd."

His fellows, in all solemnity, took up the ludicrous chorus and trumpeted in through their noses.

"Oh, whis-key's the root of all ev-il,It fills up a drunkard's hell,So why not vote out this old ev-ilAnd say farewell, whis-key, farewell!"

I smiled as I thought how little they were changed from rude retainers in an old, oak-raftered hall of feudal England. I felt as remote from civilization as though I were living behind the moat and draw-bridge of some embattled baron. In such a place anything might happen.

And then as the singers fell silent again, I became aware of a faint and distant sound of voices. The hound which lay curled upon the top step of the porch rose and sniffed the keen air, his bristles rising. In a moment he was off toward the road, barking blatantly.

The voices became more distinct and I moved from my position in the moonlight to the corner of the house where the shadow fell black enough to swallow me. As I did so a shuffling of feet in the loft told me that the men there had also caught the sound. The approaching party must be coming to this house, since we had no neighbor within three-quarters of a mile and the road ran out and ended at our gate.

Shortly a group of horsemen came into view, climbing the hill a quarter of a mile away. They seemed to be riding close together, knee to knee, and except when they crossed the intervals of the moon's spotlight one could see them only in a massed effect. They came to a halt in the shadow at a little distance from the gate.

The noiseless opening of a door and a momentary glimpse of a stealthy, rifle-armed figure slipping out into the shadow of the kitchen assured me of the preparedness of the impecunious clansmen who played watchdogs for their keep.

Then a loud and affable voice from the road gave greeting, "Hello, Cal Marcus!"

There was no immediate reply. Those inside were awaiting a more conclusive guarantee of pacific intent. Seemingly amicable salutations shouted from the night had before now brought householders into the excellent target of a lighted door, where they had lain down and died.

"Hello, Cal Marcus!" called the voice again, "we're a-comin' in."

"Who be ye?" challenged a voice from the interior. "Don't come till we know who ye be."

In the next moment I started violently and found myself in a tremor from head to foot, for the voice which answered the question was a woman's voice, and it was the voice of rich contralto which I had once heard and often imagined.

"It's I, Frances Weighborne," was the response, "and some gentlemen who rode over with me from the train." In corroboration came other voices, deep and masculine, and evidently recognized within as the voices of friends. The man in the shadow of the kitchen came out from his concealment and started down to the gate swinging his rifle at his side. A door opened and framed the emaciated, half-clad figure of Calloway Marcus. "Come right in, Ma'm," he shouted. The group rode up into the light and dismounted.

I saw her come in at the gate. The moonlight was full upon her, and I stood skulking in my concealment of shadow like a thief, held fast in a paralysis of jealousy and worship.

This was no place for me. I, of all men in the world, could least endure or be endured at that greeting between Weighborne and his wife who had ridden these mountains to be with him.

# CHAPTER XXI

## I GO WALKING AND MEET ENEMIES.

He and I had labored across those twenty miles in a wagon by daylight. I could guess what it meant at night and in the saddle—and she had done it! She had come alone, except for such chance escort as she could recruit at the mining town, and now as she walked in the moon-bath of the clearing, there was not a man of them all who carried himself with so free and unwearied a stride. She was dressed in a short riding-skirt and a heavy sweater. Her shoulders swung back as free as an Indian's, and I knew at that moment, and without doubt, that this was the elusive lady of Europe who had walked out of Shepheard's Hotel the night when I sat on the terrace. She was no fragile ornament of drawing-rooms; she was the woman who strode like a goddess and for whom timidities had no existence. She was not then, after all, I exultantly reflected, the hot-house orchid; a mere whisper and fragrance on waxy petals. She was the splendid flower I had conceived, fit for God's good open skies. And that thought sent a rich bugle note of triumph ringing through the chaos of my misery.

Of a surety it was no place for me. In what was to be said behind that door I had no part. She had come splendidly, but she had not come to me. These thoughts raced tumultuously through my mind, and when she reached the steps of the porch, and the light showed the mud and dust on her corduroy skirt, and caught the gold of her hair under an upturned hat brim, I bit savagely at my lips and turned away.

I sat for an hour or more in the shadow of a fence line, with the night mists rising and congealing under the pale moonlight like the tracery of frost on a julep mug. I had left my coat inside and at last I was conscious of being deeply chilled. As often as I turned my eyes out upon the mountain and forest they came back to dwell on the rough log wall that separated her from me. I felt the drawing of the magnet. Inside at least I could look at her, devour her with my eyes though I might not open my arms to her or even my lips except to utter commonplaces. But then the thought would come of the tenderness of the reunion which was perhaps at that moment being enacted so near me, yet so far from me, and at the picture I ground my teeth. Why had I at last discovered her to be the sum of all my dreams, and more, only to sit outside a wall of logs and know that inside she was pouring out on another man the miracle of her tenderness?

To-morrow I would deliver her husband over to her and go back. Finally, however, I realized that for to-night the Marcus house was my only available abode, and that by this time the first affections of greeting would be over. I could safely return.

Decency and civility demanded that I shake her hand and give an account of my rough nursing. The cabin was already crowded. What shifting and rearranging her arrival might necessitate was a thing to which I should accommodate myself before the household settled down to sleep. Already I might have caused inconvenience by my disappearance.

As I drew near the house, the cracks of the shutters still held threads of light. At the threshold of the room where I had left Weighborne I hesitantly knocked.

"Come in," said a low voice—her voice.

I opened the door and halted in astonishment.

She was sitting before the fire in the rough chair which was usually occupied by the old woman and her eyes were fixed on the flaring logs and the white ashes below them. She was leaning forward with her brows slightly drawn in a troubled and pained expression. The blaze threw shifting dashes of carmine on her cheeks and heightened the rose-madder of her lips. Her slender fingers were intertwined across her knees and one foot, cased in a riding-boot, was tapping the floor in evident annoyance.

Her discarded sweater hung over the chair back and against its white background her graceful slenderness was clear drawn despite the loose folds of a blue flannel shirt. The open collar revealed the arch of her throat, and though it was now circled by rough fabric instead of pearls, it was the same throat and neck that had so imperiously supported the head of the island goddess. But the deep wistfulness of her face and the troubled rise and fall of her bosom with breathing that was akin to a sigh filled me with wonder. Then the complete loveliness of her, the yearning for her swept me, and I had to grip myself resolutely for control.

I must have let myself in very quietly, for she did not turn her head. But what held me in pause and anger was the discovery that Weighborne lay asleep and breathing heavily, as though the last hours had brought no exciting incident. Could it be possible that he had slept uninterruptedly? At the thought a wave of savage resentment swept me. Had she come to me I should have arisen to meet her, though I had to shake off the sleep of death itself and push my way through the heavy weight of the grave.

I went very quietly over to her, without speaking, and still she did not raise her eyes. I looked down, cursing myself that I had dared to suspect she could burgeon only in the affluence of satins.

Slowly her gaze came up and on seeing me she gave a little start. Then she spoke in a low voice which was a trifle cool.

"Do you think your welcome is very prompt?"

I stiffened and flushed. Could she be so blindly indifferent as not to know that I had taken myself off in misery and loneliness only because I was not cad enough to intrude on that meeting? And now she permitted herself to grow piqued over the only evidence of consideration it lay in my power to show her.

"Do you think I could have done otherwise?" I inquired.

"I think if I were a man, and a woman had come across the mountains—" she halted suddenly and colored. Then she added in an altered tone of flat indifference, "It doesn't matter."

For a moment I stood there with no answer to frame. Her words bewildered me. So she might have spoken had she been free or affianced to me. I was standing above her looking down and her eyes, with the same pained wideness, were looking at some picture which the flickering flames and white embers held for her imagination. Then I understood. Her words were not after all really addressed to me. She, too, was thinking of the man asleep in the huge four-post bed who had not awakened to receive her, and upon me was falling the expression of what was in her heart because I was the only person with whom she could speak. Since he had not aroused himself she had noticed my absence. Had it been otherwise I should have been forgotten. It was the final note of my quaint and unprecedented torture that I should come in as her husband's proxy for a chiding that should have been his.

For the next few moments I stood helplessly silent. Outside I heard the distant baying of hounds off on some ungoverned chase. She sat there while the longings in my heart welled and the reason in my brain reeled, until I could feel only one thing—that she should belong to me; that my arms should enfold her—that everything which balked that end was a monstrous and hideous injustice. Then as a drunken man may suddenly sink into the irresponsible vagueness that carries him into total irresponsibility, the tidal wave mastered me. There was an inarticulate sound in my throat; something between a groan and a sob, which must have startled her, for she looked suddenly up, and as she did so I dropped to my knees beside her and carried both her hands to my lips. She flinched back with a sudden little start of astonishment, but I was now the primitive creature bereft of sanity and I gathered her to me and crushed her in my arms and covered the cool softness of her cheeks and eyes and lips with my kisses until they flushed hot and crimson. In an instant the thing was over. A wave of returning reason swept me like a sluicing from a bucket of ice-water, and I came to my feet sane and unspeakably mortified. She was still sitting very silent and her flushed color had at once died to pallor. Her eyes were wide with mystified incomprehension. Her lips moved, but shaped no words. I tried to speak, but the sense of my outrageous conduct stifled me.

She could not understand and I could not tell her, of all the torture which had so culminated. After this, even should the powers of miracle clear away every other obstacle between us, she would never listen. I heard my voice groan miserably, and with no further effort at explanation or apology, I walked, or rather stumbled, to the peg where my coat hung beside the door and let myself out into the night.

Where I went I could not say. I was tramping along with the aimlessness of the man whose steps are unguided. My one conscious intention was to keep going, to kill the rest of the night and to try, as best I might to bring myself to such a point of sanity that with to-morrow morning I could return and take my medicine with at least the dignity of the condemned criminal. Vaguely I planned self-destruction—after I had faced whatever ordeal awaited me first and I had met the obligation of supporting Marcus in court. I should tell the two of them my story and let them at least realize that before I had become the madman and the brute I had been through such things as might craze a man. Weighborne was not the sort of husband who would tamely pass without punishment such an affront to his wife and himself. I hoped that his method of reprisal would be summary. That would bring a sort of relief, yet for her sake he must let me be my own executioner, that it might end there.

The night was all a-sparkle under the moonlight, and the air, spiced with frost, went into the lungs with the tingling stimulation of needles. I tramped endlessly along the road, and all the heat of my paroxysm cooled into a chill of self-contempt. Still I had no definite idea of where I was going—I was simply plunging ahead in an effort to burn up with physical exertion the restlessness and misery that possessed me.

It was only when I had walked and run alternately for hours, frequently halting to sit by the roadside and curse myself, that I realized I must have come a long way from the house of Cal Marcus, and that the night must be well spent. I might not have even then returned to a realization of outward things had I not heard the sound of voices and the patter of unshod hoofs on the roadbed. Some roistering riders of the night were making their late way home, and had I been in a less heedless mood, Marcus' frequent injunction and the things I myself had seen would have prompted me to avail myself of the concealment offered by the fence row's tangle. But these matters were all far from my thoughts, and I merely turned back to the side to let the horsemen pass. I was walking with my head downcast at a point where the moon bathed the road, when the horses behind broke into a canter. As they passed me one of the riders, with a surprised shout to his companions, wheeled his mount to a halt just before me.

"Hold on thar!" sang out a voice. "Let's take this feller along with us."

I looked resentfully up and as I did so recognized the figure above me as that of Curt Dawson. When I met his eyes I met also the glitter of a leveled pistol.

I was in no mood to be trifled with and I knew that surrender to such a capture meant disaster to Marcus's plan of attack. Their purpose was to dispose of a dangerous witness, and since my testimony was to be damning to Curt Dawson, he above all others had a motive to serve which would make him recklessly desperate. I was unarmed, but I sprang forward meaning to strike up the weapon or force him to shoot without parley. I did not greatly care which alternative he chose, but I had no mind to be taken alive. Even if I succeeded in overpowering Garvin's gun-man, there was still his ally to reckon with. However, neither thing happened. Curt Dawson, merely laughed in his indolent fashion and jerked his horse back in its haunches, sliding from the saddle as he did so.

His fellow-traveler had now reinforced him and the two of them came over and faced me.

"Bud," said the gun-man with a slow, contemptuous drawl, "we hain't ergoin' ter kill this feller—leastways not yit. Them's the orders. He hain't ergoin' ter pester us inter hit, but we're goin' ter take him along with us. He hain't got no gun. I reckon you kin put up yours." Then he turned calmly to me and added, "Now, stranger, I low yer gwine ter come along—or get the hell of a lickin'—and then come along anyhow."

The second mountaineer slipped his revolver back into the case which, mountain fashion, he wore strapped to his side beneath his left armpit. Both men carefully buttoned their leather holsters. Meantime, I looked from one to the other, gauging their distances, and made up my mind to attack Dawson first. Then I heard the assassin calmly direct, "Now, Bud, take hold of him."

---

# CHAPTER XXII

## I FAIL TO RETURN HOME.

It was precisely as one might have given the command of attack to a dog, and under the sting of indignity, my reason once more slipped from me. I dived for Dawson and saw him reel backward under the blow I planted on his sneering mouth, but at the same instant the second pair of arms went round me from behind. Bud had "taken hold" of me and I am forced to say he did it with the effective enthusiasm of an octopus. I fancy that had there been an audience, that would have been pronounced a good fight. Sometimes the three of us swayed from side to side of the road in a triangular wrestling match; sometimes we rolled about and clawed at each other on the ground.

The moon had set and between gasping breaths, out of sweat-blinded and battered eyes, I was occasionally conscious of a steel-blue sky in which the stars seemed to dance about and of unsteady silhouetted trees. But I was more sensible of the cruel ruttiness of the road on which our feet slipped and our ankles twisted. Curt Dawson was one of those rough-and-tumble battlers who laugh as they fight. His companion kept up a running string of muttered curses, but both of them were strong, wolf-like huskies of tireless sinews and savage determination. There was, of course, no fairness of combat, but I had the advantage of trying to kill while they were fighting to take me alive, though with odds of two to one. I suppose it did not last long, but it seemed to me as interminable as the wars of Valhalla. I was very dizzy and nauseated from their kicks in the stomach and blind from blood that ran down out of a cut in my forehead—Curt Dawson wore a heavy ring—still I had the satisfaction of seeing that "Bud" was badly lamed, possibly from a twisted ankle, and that the gun-fighter himself was far from fresh. At last Garvin's head villain came into a clinch with his arms about me and under his vice-like grip I felt my ribs creaking. Bud thought me whipped and had drawn off for a moment of much-needed rest. Then I got my hands up and had the satisfaction of feeling my fingers close on Dawson's throat. The touch of flesh in my grasp seemed to rally my ebbing strength and I closed down with all the vicious force I could muster, until my nails sunk deep under the skin and his own arms relaxed and his agonized breath rattled in his windpipe. We went down locked together, but my grasp at his throat held, and as we rolled and wallowed I found myself on top and gripped the harder. I knew only one desire—to choke the last breath from his lungs, and I should have accomplished it had not the second man recognized the situation in time. If I had been fighting sanely I might have risen in time to meet him, and in his condition could have disposed of him, but I had forgotten his existence and remembered only the enemy upon whose chest my knee was pressing and whose life was fast waning under my ten clinging fingers. The mania to kill with bare hands is strong when it has once obsessed, and the second feudist found it an easy thing in my absorbed condition to throw his handkerchief about my neck and strangle me first into helplessness and finally into unconsciousness.

I came to my senses lying at the roadside, trussed up like a pig being taken to market. On either side of me lay my captors stretched at full length and resting, though a line of gray over the eastern peaks bespoke the coming of dawn, and a thin ribbon of rosy pinkness was edging the gray at the margin of the morning.

When I endeavored to rise Curt Dawson also sat up and gazed at me. His face wore scars that gave me a moment of sincere pleasure, and he found only one eye available for his scrutiny. His open shirt showed upon his neck the deep-written autograph of my finger nails, but his lips wore a grin as he reached for his broad-brimmed felt hat and placed it on the back of his head.

"Well, stranger," he drawled as good naturedly as though our combat had partaken only of elements of friendly sport, "I want ter name it to yer that you ain't noways er cripple in er fight. I told yer yer'd haf' ter come along, an' I reckon I was about right. Ef yer ready ter ride we'll heave yer up an' hike."

"What are you going to do with me?" I demanded.

"We'll figger on that by an' by," he assured me; "the fust thing we do will be plum friendly. We'll take yer where yer kin git a drink of licker."

I found that prospect grateful, for from head to foot I ached with bruises and a great weakness possessed me, but I did not propose to submit tamely at any point.

"I don't see how you are to keep me out of court unless you kill me," I suggested, "and if you are going to kill me you've got to do it here and now."

"What fer?" he queried with his tantalizing coolness. "Ef we're ergoin' ter kill yer, I reckon we'll pick our own time and place. But mebby we won't haf ter."

He rose indolently and came over with an effort to conceal the hobble of a limp, and propping my bound body against his knee proceeded to wrap his blue cotton bandana around my eyes. This being accomplished to his satisfaction, the two of them loosened my ankles and raised me to one of the saddles, leaving my hands fast bound, and passing straps around my legs. Then Dawson mounted behind me, holding me in place, for I found myself reeling feebly and in danger of collapse. The other man led the horse that carried the double burden and we started on a journey of which I have no clear remembrance, since from time to time I drifted into a condition bordering on unconsciousness.

It was full daylight but still very early when they took me from the saddle, and of course I had no idea of the road by which we had come or the country through which we had passed. The blindfold was not removed until we had entered a house and I had been helped up a steep stairway and laid on a bare, corn-shuck mattress. Then I was allowed to look on the bare walls of a loft-like room. The mattress was stretched on the floor; a tin basin surmounted a box. Otherwise there were no furnishings of any sort. Dawson was grinning down on me with a stone jug supported in the crotch of his right elbow and a tin cup in his left hand.

"Say when, stranger," he invited as he began to pour the white whiskey. "This here is your domicile fer ther present time. Yer victuals will be along presently." At the door he paused and looked back. "Ef yer needs anything," he added, "kick like hell on the flo'. They ain't nobody here that minds a little noise. The latch string hangs outside, but yer kin see fer yerself there ain't none on this side the do'."

I was for an hour satisfied to lie quietly on the mattress and rest and after they had brought me a meal of cold bread, greasy bacon and coffee, I continued inactive except for thinking. The trial was two days off and the least hardship I need expect would be imprisonment until it was over. After that I was at a loss to forecast their designs. Even then I could not be set free to tell my story, but I felt sure that nothing would be done until the arch-conspirator and dictator, Jim Garvin himself, had been consulted and had issued his imperial decree.

Shortly before noon I heard footsteps on the stairs, and since one set of feet came with the creaking caution of a person who did not wish to be heard, I feigned sleep and breathed with a deep regularity that was almost a snore. The door opened and Dawson entered. By this time I knew his delicate tread. He crossed the room and looked at me for a while, bending low down to listen to my breathing. I did not stir nor open my eyes and after a time he went again to the door and announced in a carefully guarded voice, "He's asleep all right enough."

There was no reply, so my straining ears, seeking to do duty also for the eyes I dared not open, could make no identification, but my face was turned toward the door and some inner sense declared to me with insistent conviction that the silent visitor was no other than the county judge himself. Finally Dawson turned and I counted his steps until they stopped, as I presumed, at his companion's side. At that juncture, and with infinite caution I stole a momentary peep between closely drawn lids, and the brief glimpse revealed the broad back and shoulders of the man who had so affably chatted with us at the store on the day when Weighborne and myself had arrived. Even in so cursory a survey, I knew that I was taking a decided risk, but it seemed necessary.

My room never had more than a half-light, which filtered through shutter slats so slanted that I could see nothing between them save the sky and a few stark sycamore branches. Consequently I lay in comparative darkness while they were etched against the full light of the partly open door. Now, should I regain my liberty—a thing highly improbable—I could testify that Garvin himself had knowledge of my imprisonment.

Outside my door there was silence and I told myself that they were listening. My simulated sleeping breath stole out to them and reassured them, for finally I heard Garvin's low voice. "That's the man," he said. "Just keep him here till I let you know what to do." Then their descending footsteps on the stairs drowned the words and I was once more alone.

The next day Dawson and his understrapper, "Bud," whose last name I had never learned, permitted me to accompany them to the lower floor of the house and a somewhat larger measure of freedom.

Among the many activities of his young life, Mr. Dawson had at one time enjoyed that expression of public confidence which is dear to the mountain man. He had held office as a deputy sheriff. That honor had been short-lived, but as a memento of his days of power he retained a very good pair of heavy nickeled handcuffs, and when I was made free of the lower floor these ornaments adorned my wrists. The connecting chain was long enough to give my hands a limited scope. My two jailers and myself beguiled an hour or two with a game of casino, and I was able to shuffle the cards when the deal fell to me, but the manacles were sufficiently hampering to give them a sense of entire security.

I welcomed with some eagerness an opportunity to visualize my environment, since there was now only one day left before the calling of the Marcus cases on the county court docket, and if I was to learn anything which might facilitate my escape it must be shortly accomplished.

I presumed that I had been brought to some remote and isolated point in the hills, and that even if I could rid myself of handcuffs and guardians, there still lay ahead of me the problem of a journey, probably a long one, through an unknown country.

I had still much to learn, and one of the things which did not occur to me, but which time made clear, was that Garvin never played his game twice in the same fashion. He had known that my disappearance would wake into frantic activity the smaller, but no less vigilant force of private investigators who served Cal Marcus. All the inaccessible hiding places in the heart of the timbered hills would be under espionage. He accordingly decided that the best method of keeping me under cover would be somewhat similar to that of the man in the story who knew his rooms were to be searched for a document he sought to conceal, and who adopted the method of putting it in full sight on the mantel shelf, where the searchers into corners and secret places did not take the trouble to open its envelope.

I had, in fact, been brought to a cabin which, although it nestled in a deep gorge a half-mile from the public road, and was invisible to passers-by, was still less than a mile and a quarter from the town itself. These things I was to discover on the morning of the trial when, feeling secure that it was now too late for me to avail myself of the information, Curt Dawson yielded to the temptation of informing me just how fully I had been stung.

But on my first visit to the ground floor I saw little that added to my knowledge. For months the place had palpably been swept by winds and battered by hail, tenantless and dilapidated. Indeed, the loft where I had been confined was more habitable than the lower floor. I at once recognized that they meant to leave the cabin with its air of desertion unchanged, so that any straggling investigator would pass it by with unaroused curiosity. There were two rooms, and the walls were vulnerable to windy gusts through cracks between rotting logs. The windows were glassless and an insufficient heat came from a fire which burned feebly on an open and smoke-blackened hearth. My two jailers rose constantly to fall back shivering on the jug of moonshine. There was no sign of beds or furniture of any sort. Until we arrived there the house had been abandoned.

Dawson permitted me to walk to the door and look out. The morning was gray and chilling. A slight rise in temperature had brought cold moisture and under a raw sky the hills stretched up all about us in reeking veils of foggy desolation. I saw only rattling weed stalks feeding on the decayed skeleton of what had been a fence-line before the days of abandonment, and a basin choked with volunteer timber, around which the hill-sides rose like a spite-fence, cutting off whatever lay beyond. A small front porch had graced the cabin in earlier times, but of that there now remained only one upright, and a few broken planks. I tried to locate the stable, but there was no evidence of any outhouse except some charred and over-grown timbers.

Palpably the mountaineers had not kept their horses with them. If I escaped I must do so on foot.

---

# CHAPTER XXIII

## THE OFFER OF PAROLE.

Perhaps the disappointment of my cursory reconnoiter showed itself in my expression. Curt Dawson, who stood with his arms folded and his loose length draped against the door-jamb, grinned at my dolorous face.

"Nice place, ain't hit—fer a murder?"

"That's about all," I responded affably enough. I had discovered that I was gaining nothing by a sullen attitude and I am afraid that I was even yielding to a cheap desire to impress these desperadoes with my indifference.

"By the way," I added, "what's the delay about? Why don't you finish up your job and get to a more comfortable place?"

Again he grinned. "Say, stranger," he questioned, "ain't we treatin' yer pretty well? Was you ever in any other jail where yer got better handled? I've done laid myself out ter make yer visit memorable."

"It will be," I assured him, "provided I live long enough to remember it— and—" I reached out my manacled hand for some of his "natural leaf" and loaded the cob pipe with which I had been presented, "whenever I pass through Frankfort in after years, Dawson, I promise to drop into the penitentiary and pay you a visit."

"No Dawson ain't never put up thar yit," came his quick retort, with a flash that showed I had touched his raw nerve of fear, but the smile came back as he added, "as fer me, I venerates the traditions of my family."

I had never succeeded in trapping this unique man-killer into any admission which he did not care to make, and I had begun to understand his ability to take the witness stand and run, unscathed, the gantlet of cross-examination. Still, I could not refrain now from putting a leading question.

"How did it occur to you to bring me here? Had the judge arranged in advance that I should be kidnaped?"

"The who?" he inquired.

"Judge Garvin."

"Aw!" his laugh was hearty and prolonged. "So that's the idee that's bitin' yer? The jedge thinks I'm in Virginny. In fact, stranger, I am in Virginny. I just seems ter be here, but I hain't. I brought yer here because yer'd done been firin' off yer face ter the effect that yer thought yer saw me shoot at yer from the laurel. I didn't low ter have yer testifyin' ter no sich false notion. Hit mout injer my rep'tation fer peace and quiet."

Still he later made me a proposal which I promptly rejected. "I done been studyin' right smart, an' we ain't doin' no good fer ourselves, stayin' round here," he ventured. "I done sort figgered that mebby if hits plum agreeable ter you, we mout take yer down ter the railroad cars, an' let yer promise to leave the mountings and keep yer face shet."

"What reason have you to suppose that I'd keep a promise made under duress?"

"I got two reasons ter spose hit. In the fust place the minnit yer busts yer contrack an' comes back inter this jurisdiction I gives yer my word I'm goin' ter kill yer thar same's I would er houn' dawg. In the second place, I'd have this here—" He fumbled awkwardly in his pocket and brought out a paper which he handed me to read. It was an affidavit legally drawn, with blank spaces for my signature, and that of witnesses. It purported to have been written in an attorney's office in Virginia and to be duly attested. The document represented me as stating voluntarily that I had seen Curt Dawson (in Virginia) and had realized that he was not the man whom I had recognized among our assailants. I was leaving the mountain country, so I was asked to swear, because, being an Easterner, I did not find the environment congenial. The fantastic bit of perjury culminated in this highly colored peroration:

"I feel that, in intimating that the said Curt Dawson made said or any attempt upon the lives of my party, I have been guilty of an unpardonable injustice, which I deeply deplore and for which I feel sincere chagrin." As I read that passage I laughed with an amusement that was not feigned, and then I tore the paper into fragments which I scattered among the ashes.

Dawson watched me and shrugged his shoulders.

"We don't hardly like ter kill furriners—" he said. "Them folks down below misunderstands hit an' raises hell—but I reckon ef they won't take nuthin' but killin' they kin git kilt."

So they had planned not only to keep me out of court, but to present my affidavit when it became convenient: an affidavit purporting to have been made by me across the Virginia line, while I was abjectly fleeing. Weighborne and maybe his wife as well, whom I had already grossly insulted, would hear the reading of my Iscariot betrayal. If it were possible for them to think more contemptuously of me than they already did, this would be the precise climax to bring about such a result.

Most of that day I spent below stairs. In the afternoon Bud left the cabin and shortly after returned in great excitement.

"Git that damned feller upstairs quick," he cautioned. "A couple of them Marcus men is stragglin' round here, an' they mout come in."

Dawson leaped from his chair as though electrified, and his face showed a passion of anxiety. He sprang toward me and seizing my shoulder pivoted me, pointing to the stairs.

"Hustle," he shouted as he pushed me toward the door. "Git movin'." Naturally I did not obey. I scented the possibility of rescue, so I laughed at him and stolidly stood my ground.

"This place suits me," I said.

With the swiftest demonstration of the art of weapon-drawing I have ever seen he brought his magazine pistol from its holster and thrust it into my chest. His chin shot belligerently out and his eyes narrowed into blazing slits. His profanity came in a wild torrent.

My attitude was still indifference as to whether or not I were killed. New developments had come fast since I turned from the door of the room where Weighborne's wife still sat before the fire with my stolen kisses fresh upon her lips and temples, but there had not been a moment of forgetfulness. I saw nothing ahead of me worth surrendering for, and now I felt that parlous as the situation was, it was Dawson rather than I who was frightened.

"Why don't you shoot?" I asked.

With a foul paroxysm of oaths and obscenity he threw the pistol aside, and crossing the room caught up the broken broomstick which served in lieu of a poker. I had never before been beaten. It was not pleasant, quite aside from the physical pain. And as to that phase of it, one who has not been bludgeoned with bracelets on his wrists may underestimate the actual bodily torture of the experience. At all events, I must confess that even now I sometimes awake from a nightmare in which I am being thrashed with a broomstick. I tried resistance, but one of them dragged at my chain while the other belabored me, until in a few moments I sank down in the wormwood bitterness of humiliation and defeat and was half-dragged, half-kicked up the stairs, and thrown into my room, where they gagged me against the possibility of outcry, and tied me so that I could not move from my mattress or kick upon the floor. Dawson himself remained with me. They had none too much time. Within a few minutes I heard the long-drawn halloo of persons without. The voices were friendly and the response from Bud was equally cordial. The all-pervading hypocrisy of these mountain hatreds lay over and whitewashed the attitudes of both parties. As they came they shouted their request for permission to enter, and the man inside responded with assurances of welcome. Those who were arriving were coming as spies. Those inside were bent on deceit.

We heard them calling, still from afar, that they wanted a drink of liquor, and we heard Bud shout back that his jug was at their command.

Then feet tramped about the lower floor. Curt Dawson stood back in the shadow of the eaves while this interview lasted with his weapon drawn, and never once until the visitors rode away from the house did his eyes leave the door at the head of the stairs.

When Bud came up after they had gone he was a little pale under the reaction and the strain of anxiety showed in his eyes.

"My God!" he exclaimed. "I 'lowed them fellers never was ergoin' ter leave hyar."

"What did you tell 'em?" demanded Dawson curtly.

"I told 'em I'd had a little business round hyar—let 'em think it was somethin' ter do with er still, an' said I'd jest spent the night hyar ruther then hoof hit back home."

Dawson jerked his head toward the stairway. "Did they say anythin' 'bout comin' up here?"

"No. They kinder eyed them steps, but they didn't say nothin'."

For a moment Garvin's chief henchman walked the floor, then he snarled out, "Did they ask anything erbout me?"

"Jim Calloway 'lowed that somebody'd done seed you in this country, an' I said no, that you was over thar in Virginny."

Again there was a moment's silence after which Dawson's orders came in quick staccato violence.

"Bud, you've got ter go ter town, so's they'll believe thet story. Don't come back hyar no more. Them fellers'll ride back before sundown. They suspicions somethin' an' they'll jest about slip back ter make shore. I'll take this feller an' lay out in the timber tell night. Here, give me a lift."

The two of them raised me, still gagged, and carried me down the stairs. Keeping the house between themselves and the general direction of the road, they bore me by a path that ran along a cliff to a dense clump of timber. Then the lesser villain started on with his ambling step, pausing at the cabin to pick up the jug which was to corroborate his claim that his business had to do with illicit distilling. He also stopped indoors to obliterate all traces of human occupancy.

It was perhaps a mark of respect to my belligerency which led Dawson to leave me gagged, but it was a painful compliment. He propped me up so that I might have my back against a tree, and from our place of concealment we could look down unseen on the house. This time my captor did not favor me with conversation. He sat silent with his visage black and snarling, and his hand from time to time crept involuntarily toward his holster. As for myself, I was distinctly uncomfortable. The gag cramped my jaws and the rope about my ankles was unnecessarily tight. But during the three hours that I had to sustain this position, events were transpiring which gave a certain interest to the situation. The men who had come earlier returned, as Dawson's suspicion had prophesied. They shouted as before and when they received no answer they approached with a caution that carried me back to childhood stories of Indian attacks on block houses. Finally they entered the place, and Dawson sat there looking on, his hands wrapped about his knees and his shoulders shaking with silent laughter, as he surveyed their elaborate caution. They remained in the house for more than an hour and then reconnoitered the premises, at one time passing very near our place of hiding. Once more my custodian's lean hand caressed the grip of his pistol, and his thumb slipped down the safety catch. But in the end they rode away and I sorrowfully recognized their conviction that they had been running down a false clue.

It was cold and quite dark when Dawson removed the ropes from my feet and ordered me to walk back to the house.

That night I slept the sleep of exhaustion, and it was not until my breakfast arrived the next morning that I awoke.

My captor should have left me in my loft that day and should himself have remained below where he could watch for possible intrusion. But he was overcome with a desire to talk and this impulse led to a strategic error. He wanted to point out (now that he felt certain that I could not be present when Marcus called his witnesses) how near I had been all along to the town. He described to me in elaborate detail how, were I at that moment free, I could walk in twenty-five or thirty minutes to the court-house door and proceeded to give me satirical and exact directions. He felt that he had achieved a Machiavellian victory, and it pleased him to watch me squirm with a sense of frustrated possibilities.

He even explained that while the clan was gathering he, himself, must remain away, not only because he was taxed with guarding me, but also because he was, as he facetiously insisted, "in Virginny and too fur away to git home."

"An' it's a damn shame, too," he confided, "because hit shore looks like there might be fun in town to-day. All them Marcus people is gatherin' there an' most of us fellers'll be on hand. Ef somebody gits filled up with licker thar's mighty ap' ter be a frolic. Thet co'te room hain't agoin' ter be no healthy place nohow." I shuddered. I was thinking that the woman who had come on horseback across the hills to join her husband, would probably be with him in that court-room—if he, himself, were now able to ride.

After awhile Dawson took me up stairs, and just before he closed the door, I pleaded that my handcuffs be removed, since one wrist was badly galled and lacerated. For a time he steadfastly refused, but in the end agreed to loosen the bracelet from the injured hand, and leave it dangling to the other. All morning I had been complaining of illness, and had seemed hardly able to move about. Indeed, my bruises were so apparent that I was no longer a formidable antagonist. My listlessness, in part at least, deceived him, and after the anxiety of yesterday, when his enemies were so close on his trail, he found himself in a state of reaction and buoyant over-confidence. He produced the key and fitted it into the lock of the fetter, but before he turned it he paused with a wink of self-satisfaction to say, "Jest a moment, stranger, I'll make sure of you fust."

The handcuffs were of that type which tightens with pressure as the lock tumbler slides over a series of notches. With such an arrangement the wrist can be squeezed and pinched in a refinement of torture that is disabling. Dawson now clasped his fist around the bracelet which he meant to leave locked.

"Now ef you tries to make a false move," he volunteered, "I'm goin' ter squeeze this, an' ef I has ter squeeze hit I ain't ergoin' ter loosen hit no mo'." I knew him rather well by this time and had no reason to doubt his truthfulness of intention, so I merely nodded my enforced acquiescence. I was bracing every nerve and muscle for the possible opportunity of the next moment, and at the same time was attempting to appear totally innocent of any threatening intent.

When, with his one free hand the mountaineer attempted to turn the key, something about the lock stuck, and after a mumbled oath of impatience, he bent over and took both hands to the task. That was his one incautious moment, but I stood docile while he removed the manacle, and then as he straightened up, loosely holding the chain, I sprang back, wrenching it from his grasp.

He was instantly after me, but I had put enough space between us to swing the metal weight over my head.

He saw that this time it was a fight to the death and instead of crowding in upon my blows retreated one step and thrust his hand under his armpit to the holster. But it was all too momentary even for his artistic draw. With the chain wrapped about my right hand and the left bracelet swinging free I lashed viciously out for his face—and landed. He dropped like a felled tree and as he collapsed the pistol, half-freed from its case, rattled on the floor.

---

# CHAPTER XXIV

## MY DAY IN COURT.

He was not unconscious, but dazed and groggy, and the blood was flowing from a nasty cut perilously close to the left temple. I was on him and pinning him against the planks before he could recover himself. I picked up the fallen key, liberated my right hand, then closing his manacle about his own wrist, I dragged him over to an upright post and passing the chain about it fastened his other hand. I had learned something about gagging now, so by the time he had recovered his full senses, he found himself hitched quite securely to the unplaned pillar, bootless, trouserless and speechless—but above all else astonished. I took one mean scrap of vengeance which was unnecessary. I went to the grated shutters and threw the key to the handcuffs out. Then, donning his clothes before his eyes, since my own would have proclaimed me a stranger in these parts, I turned and made my way down the stairs, once more at liberty. I did not vouchsafe him a word of farewell nor turn my head to look back, though I heard his feet pounding the floor in a frenzy of rage and futile struggle. Of course, I had possessed myself of his pistol as well as his hat, boots and trousers.

If I had needed any disguise beyond these clothes it would have been provided for me by the ragged growth of beard on my face and the unkempt hair that had not felt a comb since I left the roof of Cal Marcus. I smiled to myself as I made my exit by the broken porch and thought what his reflections at the moment must be. He was doubtless recalling his own explicit directions for reaching the court-house door. It was now between nine and ten o'clock. If I hurried there might still be time.

The town which I had seen only once before came into view as soon as I had reached the high road and made the first turn, but I was terrified to see in the distance two horsemen jogging along in leisurely approach. I scrambled across the rail fence and lay close to the earth waiting for them to pass and grudging the flight of each priceless minute. As they came nearer I heard a whining voice raised in an attempt at song.

"Right down hyar in Adamson Countee—Where they have no church of our Lord—"

Carroled one of the horsemen, and I joyously recognized the young man who, on the night of Mrs. Weighborne's arrival, had slipped out into the shadow of Cal Marcus' kitchen to reconnoiter.

In another moment I had been given a place behind the mountain boy, and soon the three of us were ambling through the squalid square of the county seat. Though groups of men stood everywhere, and eyed each other suspiciously, no one recognized, in the ragged stubble-faced wreck astride a doubly loaded horse, the kidnaped witness.

They did not take me to the court-room, but made me dismount at the back door of Cal Marcus' law office, just a stone's throw away across the narrow street. Marcus, himself, came to me there in response to a hurried summons. He listened with no show of expression or emotion and at the end of my recital gave me brief instructions, and reduced a part of my evidence to the form of an affidavit.

"Both crowds are out strong," he told me succinctly; "Garvin's gang has been instructed to start no trouble. Whether that order will stand when I spring my surprise I don't know. It will certainly be a severe test of discipline. They feel quite safe about you, and they mustn't suspect your escape. Watch that window in the court-room and when I appear and raise my hand to pour a glass of water come into court. Say nothing except in answer to my questions."

With those instructions he left me and as he crossed the alley-like space, he passed between thick clusters of mountain men who formed a practical cordon about him. I had perhaps an hour to spend alone with my eyes against the narrow slit of the slightly raised sash. I could see the lounging crowds and recognize the tensity of conditions. There was an assumption of nonchalance which sat upon these men with the stamp of spuriousness. Lines of shaggy horses hitched along two sides of the square told of many long rides. Swift, furtive glances cast backward and forward indicated the nerve strain and caution of hostile forces mingling with a show of cordiality; each bent on giving no offense, but each watchful and tightly keyed for defensive action.

A group of several young men entered the enclosure of the court-house together, and from their clothes and appearance I recognized them as the reporters from Louisville and Lexington. With the eye of the outside world upon him; with every utterance from the bench being recorded by these scribes against whom he dare not let a hand be lifted, the head of the murder syndicate must rely absolutely on chicane. He must play the fox's game and must not, under any provocation, show the wolf's teeth.

So the stage was being set, and I, waiting there in concealment, was to afford the climax of the play.

After an interminable time the lean, Lincoln-like face of Cal Marcus appeared at the dusty window of the court-room and I saw him pour a tumblerful of water from the broken pitcher. At the same instant one of the waiting clansmen threw open the door to announce, "They're callin' yer in co'te."

I needed no urging. My cue had come. They closed around me in a square and escorted me to the court-room door and as I went I heard the voice of a deputy sing-songing my name. I even imagined that in his tone was conviction that the summons would meet with no response.

In order to make clear the exact effect of my appearance, I must go back and summarize briefly, from accounts later given me by Marcus and Weighborne, the occurrences of that half-hour which preceded my calling to the witness stand.

Garvin had appeared in his court-room with his usual affability. He had even paused to shake hands with Weighborne and express regrets for his unfortunate "accident." His Honor had announced that he would prefer, in default of objection, passing all criminal cases to the foot of the docket, first disposing of several matters of probate and minor importance. To this Marcus had agreed.

When the reporters appeared the judge was surprised, but his wily composure had betrayed no evidence of chagrin, and he had halted affairs to chat with the pencil-wielders while his bailiff provided them with a table and chairs just below the rostrum.

Then had come the call of the cases against the alleged murderers of Rat-Ankle, and the attorney's prompt motion to swear Garvin off the bench. In support of his motion, Marcus launched into a dispassionate, but unsoftened charge that the judge, himself, had been the chief instigator of the ambuscade. Garvin had listened with growing amusement.

"Whose affidavits have you to file, Mr. Marcus?" he purred with unruffled composure.

"That of myself—"

"Is that all?"

"Also that of Mr. Deprayne."

"I've done been informed," drawled the Court, "that Mr. Deprayne was seen leaving for the Virginia line some days back, and that he told several people he was going home. If I'd known of his plans I'd certainly have held him as a material witness, but unfortunately it's too late now."

"Here is his affidavit," responded Marcus. "I submit it to Your Honor in support of my motion."

Garvin took the paper and read it slowly. It was in general terms and did not make clear to him that it had been so recently penned. After the perusal he delivered himself slowly.

"Learned counsel has made some mighty grave charges against this Co'te; counsel has been led astray by personal feelin'. The Co'te must protect its own dignity. The Co'te sees no reason to regard this paper as genuine, unless Mr. Deprayne himself will state that he swore to it. The Co'te regrets that it can't produce that witness for the learned counsel. The Co'te wishes only—" here he glanced significantly at the press table—"to have the full facts brought out."

"Will Your Honor," suggested Marcus, "instruct the sheriff to call Mr. Deprayne?"

Garvin had looked up with an expression of surprise and then he had smiled. "Mr. Sheriff," he instructed, "call Mr. Deprayne."

After that there had been a silence. While Garvin went through the formality of waiting to hear the announcement "the witness does not answer," he bent over the desk and once more exchanged compliments with the reporters. These scribes had been sent to expose him and he was bent on weaving about them the spell of his personality. Then it was that I entered. From the door where for an instant I halted, I took in the stained clapboard walls, carved over with crude initials; and the dingy benches full of men in jeans and hodden gray. I caught my breath as a dash of color struck my eyes and I recognized back of the gaunt standing frame of Marcus, the seated figures of Weighborne and the lady who had been so strangely important in my life. My cheeks flushed and bracing back my shoulders, I walked down the center aisle, dust-stained, with four days' growth of beard on my face, and one eye still discolored. As I came, I was conscious of a murmur of astonishment rising incredulously from the benches, and of an excited shuffling of feet.

Called out of his conversation by this sound, Garvin raised his face, still wreathed in its bland and smiling suavity—and our eyes met. For an instant I think he did not recognize me. I must have been a rather ludicrous and unprepossessing figure of a man, and possibly it was the very obvious scars of battle on my disfigured countenance that first told him my identity. At all events, the change that for an unguarded interval crossed his florid face was startling.

The smile died instantaneously and he leaned forward to stare at me as at some apparition. He quickly recovered himself, but the reporters caught the tableau of his astonishment and put a paragraph into their stories which was the preface to history-making in Adamson County.

I took my seat on the witness stand and raised my hand to be sworn, not daring to meet the eyes of the woman who sat at the attorney's elbow, though I felt her gaze upon me. Then I heard the cold modulation of Marcus's voice.

"Mr. Deprayne, state your name, age and place of residence." I did so.

"Do you aver that an affidavit charging Judge Garvin with conspiracy to murder and suppress evidence was made by you, and that it is true?"

"I do."

The shuffling of brogans and boots had died out. The fall of a pin might have been heard at the ends of the room. Every Garvin heeler and every Marcus adherent was sitting on the edge of his seat. Hands crept furtively to holsters. There was a general gasp of surprise, then as by a single impulse a number of men at one side near the back rose, and across the aisle another group came silently to its feet. The factions stood taut and motionless, eying each other with hatred. Marcus did not for an instant resume his questioning and the utter silence was as oppressive as the stillness that goes ahead of a cyclone. I knew what it meant, as every one in the room knew. The feud-factions were crouching for a spring. In another moment the ceiling might ring and rattle with the cracking of pistols and reek with the stench of burnt powder. The mountain territory has annals of such holocausts.

---

# CHAPTER XXV

## BEING LAUGHED AT.

Every one sat very still lest an excited movement or gesture precipitate the storm. From my place on the slightly elevated witness chair I had a full view of the scene in all its ominous tensity. It was as though breathing had not alone stopped, but all living animation had for the second been suspended. The body of men had been fixed as though photographed. An incautious start or the sweep of a hand pocket-ward, and the outburst would be inevitable.

There were three exceptions among those whom I may term non-combatants. One reporter began edging down behind the table. Weighborne unostentatiously shifted his position so as to place his bulky shoulders between Frances Weighborne and the crowd, and She with an impatient shifting declined his shielding and sat steadily looking to the front. She was pale, as I suppose we all were, but perfectly composed.

Then Marcus wheeled and faced the rear of the room, deliberately turning his back on the enemies who might kill him as they had killed his partner. With both hands raised above his head and his thin, cuffless wrists stretching out of his threadbare sleeves, he stood for a tense moment in silence. His rugged countenance was black with the vehemence of feeling and his deep eyes were burning.

"*Sit down!*" he thundered. He said no other word, but as he ripped out that crisp and brief command he swept both arms and hands downward, and, like hypnotic subjects answering the gesture of the demonstrator, his clansmen dropped into their seats. Garvin took the cue. He pounded on his desk with the gavel. "Order in the court-room," he shouted, and his henchmen also subsided into their benches.

A deep breath of relief swept over the place. The crisis was averted. Garvin beckoned Marcus and the opposing counsel to his side. "Gentlemen," he said coolly, "the boys seem a little excited. Unless there is an objection I'm goin' to adjourn co'te for a half-hour, and then keep this room clear of spectators." But the moment of peril had passed and when I reached the square with the attorney, who hastily spirited me out by the back door, I saw the two elements mingling with a semblance of entire peace.

Marcus took me directly to his office where we were busied with a supplemental and more exact affidavit, and I did not see the Weighbornes.

I knew that any meeting must be a most unhappy occasion, and until this matter was disposed of I was willing to postpone that final clash. We were shortly interrupted by the arrival of the county attorney, who announced that at the reconvening of court he would move to dismiss the cases. He said he realized that there could be no conviction and would not risk precipitating a conflict. Marcus could hardly refuse to allow his clients to go free, and so for the time he had to accept that surrender and reserve his ammunition for later effectiveness.

To the Marcus house we rode in cortège. I had not intended running at all, but when I came out of the law office I found that Weighborne had been much fatigued and had already started back with another guard, and I could hardly run away without facing the two of them. Marcus too, insisted that I must return, even if only for a day. Much of our business remained unfinished, and I inferred from his attitude that he knew nothing of the inevitable reckoning which I must face at the hands of my business partner. We started late and our small army arrived after nine o'clock. It was again a night of sparkle and starlight and frost. We learned that supper had been saved for us and the attorney and I ate it in silence. The Weighbornes had not waited for us. I quite understood that they might not care to break bread with me, and yet I was puzzled, because in that paralyzed moment in the court-room when I had, for the only time during the day, looked full in the lady's eyes, I had seen no anger in them. I had almost fancied that her lips half-shaped a smile. But she was a remarkable woman, and whatever her feeling, she might be magnanimous enough and big enough at such a moment, when we were all in equal danger, to lay aside for the nonce her just resentment. Now we should meet again as though that had not happened, and I had no hope of seeing her smile on me again.

Probably she had retired and I should not have to meet her until to-morrow. I rose from the table and turned to Marcus.

"Where do I sleep to-night?" I inquired.

"Your same place, sir," he answered, and when I had said good-night I turned and walked along the porch and opened the door of the room which served jointly as parlor and bedroom.

Once more, precisely as on that other night, I halted in surprise. Indeed, it might have been the other night, except that Weighborne lay where he had thrown himself down fully dressed across the big bed. But just as before, he was sleeping, and just as before She sat before the fire alone, in much the same attitude. On her face was the same trace of wistful loneliness.

I could not escape the feeling that this was in reality a part of the other evening—that it had been momentarily interrupted and that all which had transpired since I had opened this same door in this exact way, and seen this precise picture, was only the figment of disordered imagination. But it was now too late to turn back, and after all there was nothing to gain by deferring the reckoning. The three of us were here, and it would take only a moment to wake the sleeping man.

I closed the door, and my heart began the wild beating that meeting her must always bring. As I started across the room she looked up and rose. I halted where I stood, waiting for her to speak. This evening she wore a very simple gingham dress, and the chill of the room had led her to add the sweater. For a breathing space we stood there, she as slender and youthful as a school-girl; I as awkward and disheveled as a bumpkin, with my head hanging shamefacedly—awaiting sentence.

Then to my total bewilderment she smiled and held out her hand.

Had she stricken me down with a lightning bolt as the savages thought she had stricken down the profaning native, I should have been less astonished. I stood there unable to understand such forgiveness, and while I waited, she spoke.

"Now," said the voice which had been ringing in my heart ever since I had last heard it, "will you be good enough to explain things, or are you still to be the man of mystery?"

How could I explain things? How could I make a commencement? And yet it was just that which I had come to attempt.

"If I can explain at all," I said, very miserably, "it will be in one word— madness."

"Is that all?" she questioned. In her eyes was the whimsical challenge that had, on the previous occasion, swept me away from my moorings. The question that I had asked myself once before came back to my mind. Could it be that my goddess was so far from my ideal that, after all, what had occurred needed no explanation? I would not admit such a possibility, and yet her next words seemed to confirm it.

"When I first came here," she mused reflectively and only half-aloud, "you stayed outside for an hour, and then you disappeared. Of course you were a prisoner, but to-day you had the opportunity to see us. You didn't—and yet—" she flushed deeply, and I knew that her thoughts too were going back to the moment when I had, without words, avowed myself so savagely.

"I stayed out there that night," I said bluntly, "because I could hardly be an interloper, when you had ridden these infernal hills to be with *him*—" I jerked my head savagely toward the bed. Then I went doggedly on, determined that since she had forced me this far we should hereafter stand in the certain light of understanding. "I also stayed out there because, as it happens, I'm a fool. I couldn't endure witnessing a reunion between yourself and your husband." It seemed to me that she should first have called on me for other explanations.

At the last word her face clouded with an expression of absolute bewilderment, and her eyes widened as she gazed at me.

"My—my *what?*" she demanded.

"Your husband," I repeated. "Mr. Weighborne."

She contemplated me as though I were a new and rather interesting variety of maniac, then her laugh was long and delicious. Her clouded eyes cleared and danced like skies in which the sun has suddenly burst through rain.

"Oh," she said finally. "I understand now." Once more her face grew grave and she added with a catch in her voice.

"And, thank God, I *do* understand."

"For Heaven's sake," I implored, "tell me what you understand! As for me, I understand nothing."

"Why, you totally unspeakable idiot," she explained, as though she had known me always, and as though we had long been close comrades, "I haven't any husband—yet. That's my brother. Didn't you know that?"

I stood at gaze, dazed, stupefied, open-mouthed; every thing that denotes the gawky fool. Then I dropped fervently on my knees at her feet and shamelessly seized her hands in mine and kissed them. She made no effort to release them and I crushed them greedily while my tongue could find no words, until, as I afterward learned, her rings cut into the flesh.

"But," I stammered finally, "you are Frances Weighborne. His wife is Frances Weighborne. Bob Maxwell told me—"

She laughed again, and Weighborne's heavy breathing became almost a snore. After all, first impressions are best. Weighborne was a capital fellow, one could not help liking him.

"Correct," said the lady indulgently, as though she were teaching a small boy his primer lessons. "I am Frances Weighborne. My sister-in-law was also christened Frances in baptism, and acquired the surname of Weighborne in matrimony. There may, so far as I know, be various other Frances Weighbornes. We have never copyrighted the name."

"Oh, my God!" I groaned helplessly. "What an unspeakable imbecile I've been—but you're wrong, dearest, you *are* the only one."

"Do you think it necessary to swear about it?" she inquired. "And are you now quite certain that I'm the right one?"

"There isn't any time to swear," I assured her, "there is so infinitely much to say—but not here. Come out under the stars, where one can breathe. Give me five minutes. Unless I speak now I shall die of suppressed emotion. All my life I've been a supposedly extinct volcano. I'm no longer extinct." I halted my rush of words; then added, "Yes, you're the right one." I rose and, still holding her hands, lifted her to her feet. At the door, with my hand on the latch, I paused.

"No," I exclaimed, hardly realizing that I was speaking aloud. "You open it. In the dream it is always you who open the door into the other world."

She wheeled and looked me in the eyes, her own pupils wide and incredulous.

"Do you have it, too?" she demanded breathlessly. "Do you dream my dream? Do I come to you in some vague danger and lead you through a door?"

She laid her hand on the bolt, just as I had so often seen her do in my vision, and we stepped together out into the glory of the frost and moon.

"As you are doing now," I answered; then with a new wonder I demanded, "But tell me, how in Heaven's name could you dream of me before you knew me?"

She laughed mockingly.

"Perhaps," she vouchsafed, "if you make yourself very agreeable I may tell you."

---

# CHAPTER XXVI

## HOW IT ENDED—AND BEGAN.

The railings and uprights of the porch were strips of jet against a world swimming in blue and silver gray. The planks creaked under our feet. A confusion of saddles and farm gear hung against the log walls. The tin basin stood on its accustomed shelf. The world of magic was jumbled with the commonplace. I led her over to the corner where the eye could gather in the widest vista. She stood there before me very upright and slim and her eyes held mine as frankly as a child's might have done. I gazed at her for a moment more, then my arms went out and encircled her, and I talked very fast and very low.

"I may, at times, seem extremely abrupt," I confessed, "but I'm not. I've worshiped you upon a coral reef and I've made love to you through endless days and nights with stars for my witnesses much larger than these—and softer. And now I've found you—I've found you, and it doesn't matter what you say, because I shall never again let you go."

She tilted her face upward and her eyes were dancing as she quoted, "'Nobody asked you, sir.'"

She stood there, facing me, within the circle of my arms, with her chin as proudly tilted as though she were not surrendering, and with the old incomparable smile lingering on her lips.

And as I gazed at her in the witchery of the moon, the utter improbability of it all dawned upon me, until I felt that a moment would bring awakening and the old gnawing despair. The expression was that which I knew so well, and she seemed no more and no less real than she had been, looking out from the mate's chest, with the circle of mahogany-skinned savages sitting silent before her shrine.

That I had loved her was inevitable. It was written, but that was the lesser part. Here she stood looking at me out of eyes that were accepting my love without question. Why did she, without even the siege of a long wooing, so permit me to step into the temple of her life, as naturally as though it were the shrine of the coral island where I belonged as high-priest and demi-god?

She had, before to-night, met me only once, and then I had been the churl, brusquely rebuffing her sweet courtesy. Yet she had ridden across the hills, and something sang to me that it was to me she had ridden, though she may have called it coming to her brother. Why was it? Had I really conjured her soul to me by wishing it across the world? Had supreme forces compelled us both, so that preliminary details were superfluous between us?

However that might be, the gracious smile died slowly on her lips to a seriousness far sweeter, and as she looked into my face her eyes widened, and dropped all concealment until I was gazing into her soul.

When a woman meets the eyes of a man in that fashion he ceases to question, and wishes only to do reverence. It is like rolling back the waters of the sea and revealing the wonders of the deeps. For it is decreed that the eyes of a woman are given her in defense, to hide behind their dance and sparkle the things which lie beneath—and to disarm. When once they have opened in the miracle of self-revelation and surrendered their secret, one must be unworthy who feels himself worthy of such a manifestation.

And the secret I read there was that she loved me beyond all doubting. It mattered no longer how the wonder had come to pass. That was a mere point of god-craft. It had happened, and the stars were singing.

I dropped on one knee and lifted her hand to my lips.

Later, I sketched rapidly, agitatedly, the story of the coming of her portrait to the island, of its place on the chest and its subsequent worship. I told her of meeting Keller on the steamer and Maxwell in New York. I summarized the chain of evidence which had to my mind proved her to be Mrs. Weighborne. I have no doubt that I told it badly, but that was of no consequence, since back of my broken narration was the pent-up rush of emotion, and to her this seemed important. Nor did my story, so fantastic that I hardly expected her to accept it without proof, seem to surprise her.

"And," I concluded, "I am going to build you a new temple which will make the Taj Mahal a tawdry mosque, for every block and rafter will be love, and each year we live I shall add new minarets of worship—and not only five times each day but a hundred, its *muezzin* shall call me to prayer."

Her eyes were glowing, and her laugh trembled.

"I came quite a long way," she told me, "to make you say that, but after all you have done it very nicely."

"But," I admitted after a long pause, "I don't yet understand—not that it matters now—but why? That word is beating at my brain—why in the names of all the gods should you care?"

"Why shouldn't I?" she indignantly countered.

"You have known me," I said blankly, "a few days—and I should have imagined that I made a sorry impression."

She laughed again.

"I have known you always," she replied.

I shook my head wonderingly.

"Listen," she commanded. "Once upon a time—that's the way all fairy stories start—I saw you. You didn't notice me much. I was just a kid, but I fell in love with you. To be exact, it was ten years ago this month."

There was no end to wonders. All the loose threads of coincidence were being plaited into a single cable, and the cable was my life line.

"As I grew up I met a lot of men and they insisted on saying nice things to me; but they were all things of one kind and that wasn't the kind I wanted—besides, you see, I was waiting. I knew that some day you would come and that if you had anything to say it would be different. I compared them all with you. It wasn't just a girl's romantic foolishness. There was destiny in it. You know the Moslem text—'man's fate is about his neck.' You had no chance to escape me."

"I, too, knew it was written," I told her, "but I was afraid we should meet too late. When I saw you at Lexington I thought it was too late."

"I was never afraid of that," she affirmed. "Sometimes I have known that you were in danger—and later I've known that you escaped. Then there was the dream—the one dream about the door that came over and over.... At times it seemed that you were very near. Once at Cairo I felt that I was going to meet you around some corner or in some bazaar—but I didn't."

"You might, if you had turned your head," I declared. "Did you by any chance lose a diary at Cairo?"

This time it was she who was surprised.

"I lost one somewhere," she acknowledged; then as she colored divinely she demanded, "You didn't find it, did you? You didn't read those fool things?"

"It wasn't foolishness," I quoted. "There was destiny in it." And then I made full confession.

"I'm glad you wrote it," I added. "I owe that diary something and I want all my debt to be to you."

For a moment she was silent, then she looked up again and confronted me once more with a charge of stupidity.

"And you read that, and knew what football game it was, and yet you never recognized yourself! What are your brains made of, anyway?"

How could a man reply to such a sublime absurdity as that? I groaned.

"In the diary you wrote of an apotheosis," I confessed. "How in the name of all that is logical could I connect myself with this admirable, impossible superman? You failed to give the name."

She looked at me and laughed.

"The man is also modest," she observed.

"Of course," I demurred, "it's great to see you treading the clouds, with ideals for your playmates. Moreover, it's appropriate; but I'm down here, you know, earthbound and extremely mortal. If we are to walk together you must come down and join me."

"I'll take you up with me," she hospitably asserted, and though since then she must have discovered many times that she had draped her cloth of gold upon a lay figure and had made a plumed and mailed knight of a failure and an inconsequent, yet she has, with gallant stubbornness, refused to admit it.

"Dearest," I said very humbly, "I have been inconceivably boorish, and worse. How could you bring yourself to forgive it?"

"Because," she answered, "I'm a woman—and inquisitive. I knew how you felt, and I wanted to find out why you acted so horridly at Lexington."

"I was trying very hard not to tell you how I felt," I admitted.

"You didn't have to tell me—in words," she laughed. "You told me in a hundred other ways, that were just as plain."

"Then the only part of my story," I said, a little crest-fallen, "which is new to you is the information that you were a goddess and I a high priest, out there in the South Seas?"

"Oh, that wasn't new at all," she ruthlessly enlightened, "I knew that, too."

"Is there anything you don't know?" I inquired. "What gift of prophetic vision—"

"There wasn't any vision about it," she interrupted. "I got a letter from Mrs. Keller the day before you reached Kentucky. I guess when you get back to New York you'll find one from the captain. His wife wrote to tell me you were coming. That was why I got a headache and stayed at home that night."

She laid her hand on my forearm. My sleeves were uprolled to the elbows.

"Dearest," she exclaimed in sudden anxiety, "you're cold!" I suppose I was, but I had not known it.

---

It has been some time now since I have written in the diary which had its birth under such strange circumstances. The narrative went into a pigeon-hole because I have been too busy living to think of reflecting upon life. It was a device for moments of emptiness and in later times also for moments of extraordinary jubilation, but since the last pages were scribbled there has been enough of celebration in merely living out the days. Yet now I must add a postscript, so that some time He may have the full record before him. He is my little son.

He is teaching me a great many things and finding in me a willing pupil. When I first walked out into the public ways after his entrance to the stage whereon I hope he will be cast in a worthy part, I walked differently. I walked with the pride of an emperor. Not the pride of arrogance. I needed no car of ivory and bronze with captives marching fettered at its wheel. I needed no slave to whisper in my ear, "Remember, Cæsar, thou art but a man." I was filled with a new graciousness and wished to be generously courteous to all men, yet that desire was born of a sense of vast superiority. I had found the meaning of life; the secret of which the gulls shrieked in mating-time around the rocks of the island—though then my ears were deaf to its significance.

She has minted from the precious metal of her soul a life which, with the other lives of his day, will form the mosaic of his times. I have the prospect before me of new miracles as that new life unfolds. I feel the exaltation of being undeservedly linked with something vastly greater than myself. I made an awkward effort once to put some part of this idea into words, but Frances only laughed. To her it is all quite natural. Her only comment was that he is as much mine as hers, which was a flattery that even my egotism could scarcely assimilate.

We have not named him yet, but an idea struck me a day or two ago while I was sitting at my down-town desk, and I straightway called her up.

"I have just thought of a name," I said. "I want to call him Francis Ra-Tuiki. Of course," I hastened to add, realizing that the silence at the other end of the wire threatened protest, "of course we can dignify it with highly unphonetic spelling, if you like."

"I don't know," she judiciously reflected. Then with a sudden afterthought she added, "That might possibly do for a middle name. I have already decided upon the first."

I wonder what name she has in mind—and she had just finished telling me that I had a full half-interest in that kid!

A railroad now runs into Adamson County and the new order is replacing the old. My wife and I and our brother went down on the first train run over the new line. The people had gathered to see the spectacle, and incredible as it may seem, there were among them some who looked for the first time on a locomotive. Old Mrs. Marcus, a little more withered and monkey-like, was there, and as she contemplated the marvel she could only murmur in wonderment, "Well, Provi-*dence*!"

Calloway Marcus no longer rides in a hollow square, but goes openly to court to defend the railway's damage suits. Yet now that the law is becoming adequate, he will never have the opportunity to turn it, as his weapon of reprisal, against Jim Garvin. Retribution came to the head of the murder syndicate with grimmer and more appropriate drama than Marcus had planned. The judge fell behind his own counter, riddled with bullets bought from his own shelf, and fired by the hand of his own chief henchman and jackal.

Though one of the last of the terrorized juries sat in the box, to the end that the slayer "came cl'ar," it is now Curt Dawson who goes sunken-eyed and body-guarded, searching the shadows. Shots from the laurel are few— but occasional even now—and Garvin's boy is nearing manhood. At all events, Garvin's executioner seems convinced that reprisal will come to him. Perhaps it is a premonition.